Legends

A Literary Journal from
Grey Wolfe Publishing

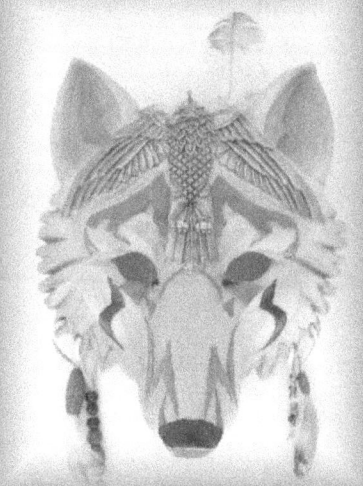

Winter 2014

Edited by Diana Kathryn Plopa
and Jennifer Koch

Grey Wolfe Publishing, LLC
PO Box 1088
Birmingham, Michigan 48009
www.GreyWolfePublishing.com

© 2014 Grey Wolfe Publishing
Published by Grey Wolfe Publishing, LLC
www.GreyWolfePublishing.com
All Rights Reserved

ISBN: 978-1628280289
Library of Congress Control Number: 2014939153

Legends

Grey Wolfe Publishing's
Quarterly Literary Journal
Winter 2014

Edited by Diana Kathryn Plopa
and Jennifer Koch

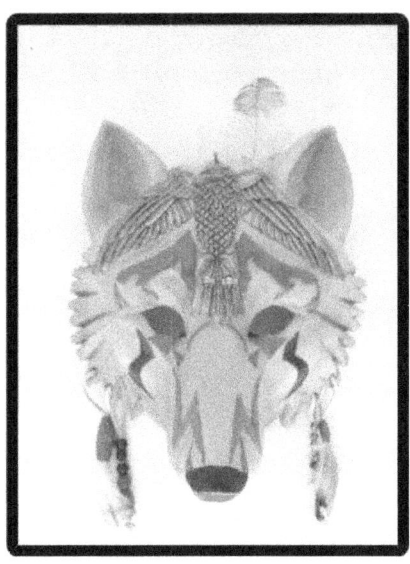

Legends is a quarterly literary journal produced by Grey Wolfe Publishing.

Four times a year, talented writers from around the globe lend their work to this showcase of short stories, essays and poems for your reading enjoyment.

Some of the stories and poems within these pages may help you revisit memories you thought you'd forgotten. Others may reawaken emotions long dormant. And still others may reacquaint you with the laughter of your childhood. Regardless of which piece of poetry or prose you find most appealing, we are certain that these authors will quickly become some of your new favorites.

Grey Wolfe Publishing is an independent publishing house, headquartered in Michigan. We are committed to walking through the paths of the publishing forest with our authors as equals; never leading, never following… always side-by-side, with the strength and confidence of the Pack.

Ni Bóna Na Coróin.

Acknowledgements

The production of this book each quarter could not be accomplished without the expertise, literary passion and dedication of our amazing Pack. Each is a writer as well as a company team member; and each lends their unique perspective to serve both the company and our authors with integrity and creativity. We are grateful for their daily contributions to the growth of the Pack.

Contents

Contributing Authors   **Page 185**

1.
A Quaff Of Hope
Yasmin Kahn

The reflection of her bloodshot eyes
In the transparency of her fate's demise
Gulping down the remnants of anguish
The lump in her throat still did languish
Rising to a cry that could not be heard
Knotting down in her stomach that she could not purge
She could not let herself drown in her sorrow
Some part of her still hoped for a better tomorrow
Anticipation tantalized, teased her forlornness
Soothing to ease her sense of wretchedness
Her reverie vitalized her sagging spirit
Surpassing any disillusions decrepit
Vitality of her soul's essence roused her optimism
Flooding her being with newfound enthusiasm.

2.
Aeolian Drifts
Joann Grisetti

the first fall of winter begins
the frisky Aeolian drifts
watching in awe, my spirit lifts

silver sequined the snowflakes spin
through branches bare and charcoal grey
past the chattering of blue jays

one lost flake on uncovered skin
melts slowly and deliciously
unleashing all the memories

swirling around me all his kin
covering asters' one last bloom
shrouding the world in frozen gloom.

in childish joy, I start to spin
and dizzy fall onto the snow
thereon to bask in bright moon glow;

the first fall of winter begins
silver sequined the snowflakes spin
one lost flake on uncovered skin
swirling around me all his kin
in childish joy, I start to spin.

3.
A Few Innocuous Lines
Sarah Z. Sleeper

Alice let her eyes go blurry and listened to the rough and melodic sound of Mikhail Gorbachev's voice, letting it flow over and around her without hearing most of the words. When he'd first started speaking that night, Alice had leaned in, as if moving six inches closer to the enormous stage would allow her to better hear his voice, which was already being projected by the highest of high-tech sound systems. After a few moments, she settled back in her chair.

He droned on about software, social networking, and enterprise accounting. Of course, these were the topics of the conference and the reason that five-thousand people had come to CNN Center in Atlanta. Black, grey and, blue-suited sales men and women, vice presidents and marketers, all sitting with tipsy smiles on this January night, waiting for the speech to end so that more drinking could commence. Drinking, the real reason people go to conferences, Alice thought. Her black leather briefcase rested heavily on her leg, and she contained the urge to kick it.

She couldn't stop staring at Gorbachev's wine stain, clearly visible in the spotlight from her third-row seat. It looked purple and painful on his broad forehead, and she wondered if he had ever considered having it removed, or burned off, or whatever a dermatologist would do to make it disappear. Maybe he felt it was a badge of his communist upbringing, a visible sign of stoic tolerance and devoted non-self-interest.

"The world is a rapidly changing place with ever-expanding borders of commerce and culture," Gorbachev concluded, to over-generous applause. As she gathered her laptop and purse, it struck Alice as absurd that this big-time, Cold War communist, former leader of the Soviet Block, had been reduced to giving tepid closing keynote speeches. She wondered when this participant in twentieth century History with a capital "H" had sold out and become a guy who got paid to talk to computer hacks.

And Alice thought it was equally silly that the Wall Street Journal had flown her here to cover this event. She knew the paper was desperate for something new about business in Russia, especially as the Sochi Olympics drew closer, but it was clear this trip would not deliver and was, in her opinion, a waste of time and money. There had been nothing of substance in what Gorbachev said. She had counted on gleaning material for her story from a promised interview. But right before the speech, Gorbachev's press agent, George, had made up an excuse about a plane to catch.

"Mr. Gorbachev sends his apologies," George had said to her. "He will be happy to speak with you at another time in the very near future." George winked when he said that. Such formal phrasing accented by such a casual gesture. Alice found his English accent charming and knew that it cushioned the otherwise lascivious effect of his flirtation. Now Alice would have to write the story based solely on the boring speech.

She couldn't help thinking that George's head was both strange-looking and attractive, kind of pretty in its perfect round shininess. He wasn't handsome, but was at least interesting, with a face that moved and restructured itself, especially around the eyes, as he talked. His eyes, hazel-green and deep-set, seemed to disagree with what his mouth was saying. "Oh I'm sorry," he'd said, and his eyes had been wide open like he was about to laugh. "We'll do it another time soon, I promise," and his eyes looked sideways toward the exit.

Alice headed toward the exit with the lines of computer lemmings. She decided she would find a way to paraphrase Gorbachev so he didn't sound so dull-witted in print. Alice pondered the snarky questions she would have asked. "How does it feel to be a double-C, a 'Capitalist Communist,' paid five dollars per word to give mundane lectures? Oh, and how much money did you have to pay the Russian mob last year?" How she would have loved to ask him those questions.

Alice walked fast toward her hotel, hustling to get to the safety of her room and out of the bustling, Friday-night street, crowded despite the icy sidewalk and snowfall. She would float into her soft hotel bed, with its overstuffed pillows and extra-comfy comforter. Downtown Atlanta was filled with a scary parade of tattered bums, disheveled college boys and tired, half-drunk business men. The moonlight, weirdly bright, made the people she passed look ghostly and unnaturally large, lit up and with exaggerated stature.

Five more minutes and I'll be at the Omni, she thought, and then she saw George, on the sidewalk ahead of her, turning into a brightly lit doorway. It was impossible to miss his bald head, so compact and circular on top of broad shoulders. Definitely more going inside that round head of his than he was willing to say out loud.

She pulled out her phone and made a quick goodnight call to Mike. He was already in bed back in their New York apartment. "Sure sweetie. Tell me about Gorbachev tomorrow, okay? Love you," he murmured. Her feet ached from her business pumps, and she felt a blister forming on her heel. Her briefcase felt like a sack of ice, and she yearned to drop it on the sidewalk.

Alice had met Mike at the Journal and found they were kindred spirits, intellectuals and hard workers. They'd bonded over late nights, coffee and deadlines. They both tended to over-research their subjects and over-interview their sources. Each erred on the side of too much information-gathering, never too little. Neither was willing to risk making a factual mistake, or missing a key point that would provide crucial context. They were dedicated to context—never presenting a data point without enough accurate contextual information to make its relevance clear. They had begun their romance by waging a bet about who could keep the corrections column editor at bay longest, and for seven years they had a tie. Not bad, seven years without a substantial error, but then two months ago Alice had omitted the word "not" and no one had caught it until it was too late. "Russian officials claim they do abuse convicted felons," was published in a page-two article. Alice had to make a slew of apology calls. The paper printed a correction. Most irritating to Alice was that Mike never mentioned it; he was too kind to rub it in.

It wasn't Alice's plan to go to the bar that night. She wasn't really the type who went to bars alone. She was more of the in-bed-by-a-decent hour type, even when she was on reporting trips. Hoping maybe she could pin him down for a reschedule, Alice followed George into the packed watering hole. And it was fair to call it a watering hole. Lou's Lounge had bright "Miller" and "Coors" signs that flashed red in her face as she walked in. It was packed. People in candlelit booths, dozens of bodies perched on bar stools, jazz-pop sifting from a juke box, a mixture of bourbon and aftershave hanging in the air. Mostly conference goers, Alice assumed, there to wind down from the week.

She removed her coat and draped it over her briefcase. She could use a wind-down herself after her hectic week—a few days at The Hague, then this forty-eight-hour turnaround to Atlanta. She'd had deadlines each afternoon, five or more interviews every day, each one painstakingly transcribed so she wouldn't miss any gem of insight or information. And now, the jewel interview with Gorbachev, not happening. It was beyond frustrating.

Alice spotted George sitting alone in a booth. She went over. "If I buy you a drink will you get me an interview tonight?" She flashed him her most persuasive smile.

"If you buy me a drink, I'll make up some quotes you can use." His eyes were slits, as if asking her to conspire with her in something undefined and sordid.

She sat down in the booth across from George, her hands folded in front of her on the table. He reached across the table and put both of his hands on top of hers. She was surprised by this too-familiar gesture, and it gave her stomach a jolt. "Alice, you know I'd do anything to help you." He looked flatly into her eyes, unblinking. She perceived some underlying meaning, some significance to his statement that she wasn't quite catching on to.

So okay. He's going to hit on me. I can handle it. When the waitress approached, she took her hands out from under his. She had liked the weight of his hands and the feel of them. They were warm, soothing. She was not surprised that he had a strong grip.

Alice had dealt with George many times over the years, and he had always been a congenial press agent, doing his best to help her find the right sources. They had dinners together, in groups, five or six times, but she never sat this close to him before. She had been careful about appearances so that she was above reproach, and she never gave his story ideas precedence just because George was a nice guy.

"You know, you're attractive for a reporter." George came over to Alice's side of the booth and slid in beside her.

Alice turned away, too self-conscious to look at him. She hoped her hair hadn't been flatted by the wet snow, so odd for Atlanta, and she wondered when she'd last put on lipstick. After a long, silent pause, she turned and looked straight at him, eyebrows raised. "Well, you're not so bad yourself. But really, is this what it is? Tipsy flirtation at Lou's Lounge? Aren't we supposed to be serious news people?"

George smiled, a small, one-sided smile, while his eyes remained steady, serious. From this vantage and in this dim light, she could see that they were darker green and slightly droopy on the outside corners, no hint of smile. "Serious? You take all of this seriously? Well, I wouldn't have figured you for so provincial or proper."

Her suit jacket felt binding and she slid it off, dropped it over the coat on her briefcase. She knew he was right. She was a study in responsibility. She had graduated from Northwestern J-school with top honors and got a plum job as foreign correspondent, covering Russia. Her byline hit the front page several times a week. She was known for taking on assignments that required grueling hours and frantic deadlines, and for her spot-on prose. Alice could make pedantic points and arcane facts sing and transfigure themselves into compelling stories, with beginnings, middles and powerful endings, not endings that dribbled out into the inconsequential as so many newspaper stories did. In fact, George had once complimented her on a story about Vladimir Putin. Instead of the usual rigmarole about how he was in bed with corrupt companies, Alice had written a piece analyzing his psychology—how a small-stature boy, a political climber from St. Petersburg, grew into a fierce and feared president. She had interviewed his grade school teachers, his neighbors, psychologists and a spate of leadership experts, and found a story no one else had done. George had called to congratulate her when she won an award for the story. "Well done. Ms. White. Putin will be put out. Perfect execution." Now, sitting here with George at this dark and crowded bar, she felt guilty, sort of slippery and shadowy.

"Mike, that's your husband, right?" George must have been reading her mind, knowing that she was feeling a twinge of guilt, even though, so far, she hadn't done a single wrong thing. Alice slid away from George, down the bench, trying to take charge of the conversation. "How's life with Gorby? Do you like working with him?"

Frowning, George answered, "No interviews for you." Again, he winked, just as he had done earlier that day. And just like before, the rest of his face didn't comply. His mouth was tight and turned down. "Ah, here are more drinks." The waitress deposited another martini in front of Alice, and something brown, scotch maybe, in front of George.

"Look George, I don't really want..." Alice gazed out toward the crowded dance floor, unsure of what she wanted to say. She stood up and managed to step over George to exit the booth. The front of her thigh rubbed across his knee and she flushed. She was glad it was too dark for him to see that.

"Look, I'm going to pack it in for the night. George, thanks for the drinks. Let me know if we can do that interview sometime. I'll write another story if we can lock down Gorbachev."

But as she turned to go, George stood and took hold of Alice's arm, a gentle but unrelenting grip. "Don't forget your briefcase," he said, narrowing his eyes and moving closer to her. Alice felt a bit queasy, unsteady on her feet. What the hell am I doing here anyway?

She flashed back to Mike, home in Manhattan, tucked in bed. "C'mon. Stay a little longer. Let's dance," George whispered, taking Alice by the hand, guiding her through the swaying bodies. Again she felt his pleasant warmth and his strength, radiating into her hand from his. He placed her briefcase on the floor next to them and they danced around it, sometimes bumping it with their shins.

Heat built up on the small of her back where George's fingers had settled into the bones and curves of her lower spine. She wondered if she could get away with a kiss, nothing sexual, just a first kiss with a new kisser, not the familiar, same-for-the-last-eight-years kisses she shared with Mike.

Tilting her face up, eyes half opened, Alice noticed a small jagged scar under his eye. She'd never seen it before, not in the three years she'd worked with him. It was tiny, a half-inch zigzag under his left eye, the skin surrounding it whiter than the rest.

"Where did you get that?" Alice slurred, but George didn't answer.

The song ended. Alice stepped back, out of George's grip. People were clearing off the floor, but she didn't move. A shift of acquiescence and acceptance washed over Alice. Her spinal column felt as flexible as her eyes were bleary. She had a foggy recognition that she should try to break the spell, and so she averted her eyes, looked at her briefcase on the floor, realized its smooth black leather would be tacky and dirty from sitting on the sticky black tile, filthy with spilled liquor and littered with dropped cocktail napkins.

The waitress emerged through the crowd and put another drink in Alice's hand. Alice sipped the martini without tasting it, feeling it slide into her belly, its heat spreading to her limbs and igniting her cheeks. Her mind felt as mushy as her body, wavering, unclear.

The music started again, soft, a blues song, volume low on the juke box. George's hand returned to Alice's back. Pins poked at her nerve endings, but she also felt comfortably drowsy, moving with the music, following George's lead. On the fringe of her awareness she recognized how uneasy it made her feel to be so out of control, just along for whatever ride George wanted to take her on. But she pressed herself up to George, tightly enough to feel his lean muscles and smell the scotch on his breath. They danced this way for several songs, pausing a couple of times to drink more. Drunk. I am definitely drunk.

The room was getting smaller, closing in on her. She pushed away from George and slid into the closest empty chair. The other patrons faded out of her view and she knew she was either going to throw up or pass out.

"Don't worry Alice. I'll take care of you." The last thing Alice remembered seeing was George's wry smile. At the same time, she felt his hands grab hold of her arms, lift her up and start moving her toward the door.

Alice awoke to find her mouth was sandpaper. She swallowed hard and pain shot through her parched throat. She opened her eyes, and struggled to see where she was. She recognized her black briefcase, sitting on a wooden luggage stand, and her wool coat and suit jacket draped over a chair. Thank goodness! I'm in my room. What the hell happened?

She reached for a glass of water on the bedside stand and sipped, grateful for the cool liquid on her raw lips. She sat up, her head cobwebs and dully buzzing, and saw him, George, sitting on an ivory couch nearby, watching her. "Here, take these," he said, handing her two aspirin. "When you feel better, I have an appointment for you."

Oh God. Did I sleep with George?

"Alice, you're fine." George sat on the edge of the bed. "Nothing awful happened. You got sick and I brought you back here."

She squeezed her eyes shut, and when she reopened them, George was still there. Her head felt like it was about to explode, and Alice jerked, now fully awake.

"C'mon. Can you get up? We need to hurry," George stood, apparently expecting her to do the same. "The interview, Alice. I got you the interview. But we have to do it now. He only has a few minutes."

Alice looked down, realized she was still in her black suit, her legs still wrapped in too-tight leggings. "Okay." She forced her brain to snap into work mode, shuffled to the bathroom, brushed her teeth, smoothed her hair. Her makeup was still in place, even her lipstick. She grabbed her briefcase; inside were her voice recorder and notes. George led her down the hallway, up the escalator, into the presidential suite. There sat Gorbachev, portly in a big yellow velvet armchair, the purple mark on his head dark against the icy sun that shone on it through a large picture window.

"You wanted an interview." Gorbachev spoke quietly, calmly. "So here I am. Please sit," he said, indicating the matching yellow velvet chair next to him. "We have to take precautions before granting you access. We just want to interview you." Gorbachev smiled. Alice noticed that he was wearing the same blue pin-stripe suit he had on at his speech the night before.

"What are you talking about?" She shivered as she spat out the words. "I'm supposed to be interviewing you. You don't interview me." She attempted to stand, but her legs were unstable. She slumped into the chair. George came over and put one hand on her shoulder. She flashed back to his embrace on the dance floor and his grip as he held her.

"Mrs. White," Gorbachev said, "I am sorry for the precautions George had to take in getting you here. I couldn't meet with you at the conference because it was too public. Let me now speak plainly."

Alice squeezed her eyes shut and inhaled. When she opened them again, she was still in the same room with the same groggy, aching head, the same surreal situation. She saw a Monet reprint above the armchair where Gorbachev sat, only it was hung upside down, its hazy, indistinct flowers not reaching upward toward the cloud-speckled sky, but arching toward the royal blue hotel carpet.

"I'd like you to work for me," Gorbachev continued. "I've followed your Journal work for years. I could really use you on my team." His thick accent made the word team sound like tee-ahm. "It's not spying or anything so dramatic. We don't do that anymore. Not since the Cold War ended." He put four fingers up in the air when he said that, making air quotes around the word "ended."

"I'll pay you three times as much as you make now. No one will ever know. You will have complete security and anonymity." Gorbachev stood. Watching him made Alice dizzier. He was much fatter close up than he had looked from a distance.

"All I need you to do is include a few lines in your articles, the one you are working on now as well as others you will do in the future. Just a few innocuous lines, some words about how well the Russian economy is doing. Just a small number of well-placed phrases in each of your pieces that mention Russia, our people or our companies."

Alice was worn around her edges, still drugged and confused. Last night, she had been willing, with George, anyway. In the swaying, warmth of his hug in that bar, her upright stance had softened. Processing what Gorbachev said, she sat like a mound of soiled laundry on the edge of the chair, only her eyes moving from him to George, who sat a loveseat across the room now, looking at her with open-eyed expectation—the first time she could clearly read his expression.

Back home, Mike asked her about the trip. "What was the highlight? Did you see George?" He hugged her close, as if somehow he knew. Their tidy kitchen looked remarkably tiny and sterile in the bright wash of morning sun.

"No highlight really," she said, willing her body to soften in his hug. "The snow made everything weird."

"Yeah. Some kind of freak weather," he said. "Glad you made it home." He looked at her with eyes full of such sincerity and concern that she wanted to wince. She instead turned her attention toward the coffee pot on the counter.

"The speech was a dud and the interview got cancelled. I cobbled together a piece on the speaking circuit for former world leaders, you know, how they get gigs, how much they get paid, that sort of thing. I don't even know when it will run."

"Did you see that story in the Times yesterday?" Mike shook his head and Alice saw his genuine disgust. "The one about that reporter who fabricated something like half of his stories? Can you believe it?" Alice saw that Mike was appalled, his lips pursed, his head shaking back and forth in disapproval, not a strand of hair moving on his close-cropped cut. She flinched and looked toward the window, for the first time noticing an indented thumbprint in the new beige paint on the sill. The contractor must have been careless in his rush to perfect the upgrades they had scrimped to afford.

She sat at the kitchen table, not answering, just breathing in the pungent, earthy smell of her coffee. Her skin felt new, soft and translucent, as if her guts and heart could revolt and make their way through and jump outside her body. It would take some time to get used to being this new Alice. The boundaries and rules around which she had framed her career and life were still solid, but her own defining lines had become squirmy and shifty. The choices, so many choices! Her options felt endless, stretching out before her like a freshly asphalted city street, and she its solitary pedestrian, alone, for better or worse.

4.
Announcing The Gravel Mountain Ski Patrol Newsletter
Earl W. Wolfe

Our Area Manager again brought to our attention his unhappiness with the spill-over resulting from the inspired humor and the gentle pranks that members of the ski patrol have been enjoying with the ski instructors and some of the customers. This has negatively affected various members of the management team and the sales of tickets. The owner is unpleased with the loss of revenue. Your executive committee, chastised, was told to publish a newsletter that would inform us of the proper attitude and professional conduct that the area management expects from the patrollers; nay, demands of us. This is the first one.

A discussion was subsequently held by our executive committee and a motion made and seconded that ended up with me being railroaded into the position of editor of THE GRAVEL MOUNTAIN SKI PATROL NEWSLETTER. I did my best to avoid this undesired occupation, but I was the only one who had a computer with word processing and spel chek (sp?) and the only one who had a rudimentary understanding of the "point and punch" method of typing. Other reasons: I have been temporarily sidelined from regular patrolling after receiving a tear in the right sleeve of my patrol jacket, I allowed my toenails to grow and my ski socks have holes in their toes, and I didn't buff out the scratch on the top of my left ski. These items would not normally have forced me to accept this position, but I am between girlfriends who have the necessary skills for repairing these concerns, and I have a hangnail. So here I am, the editor.

Your unhappy newsletter editor pleads that you understand that he is simply the messenger of any management generated comments, still remains a true-blue patroller and will be back in the pack as soon as a loving, lively and likely lady with the proper skill set appears on the scene. I am currently holding interviews with all applicants at nine-thirty every Friday evening. I am interviewing applicants at the far corner of the lounge at the table with subdued lighting overlooking the central fireplace and the slopes.

Now, one of my own concerns: Some of you - taking umbrage at my new, but forced, position and loudly denouncing me as a traitor - frosted the windows on my car. You will hopefully rue this action now that you know that I was railroaded. I bet that it took at least two large packages of Oreos to accomplish this sugary feat and I too, would feel badly about the unnecessary wasting of the best part of the cookies. Our Patrol Director's dog evidently found and ate all of the now frostless cookies because he regurgitated the evidence all over the brand-new white carpet in the manager's office. Our patrol was charged with causing the damage and the carpet cleaners were necessarily paid by a disbursement from our party fund. They had a set price: four rooms for $100.00. They subsequently redid the carpet in the manager's office three additional times and did remove 80% of the worst of the chocolate brown and bile green stains. Hopefully, mud tracked in by employees or customers will eventually disguise the damage so that the manager will, in time, forgive and forget.

This just across my desk: The avalanche cannon that was lost has been found, but the explosive rounds are, perhaps, missing. There are reports that the rounds were, perhaps, used to make some improvised explosive devices (IEDs). They may, perhaps, have been manufactured then secreted, stashed or buried around the ski area and the buildings. We strongly suggest that all patrollers walk carefully and gingerly around the area, or that they get an unassuming or naïve ski instructor to walk ahead, id est., to "break the trail" in unmarked areas. An eight to ten foot lead should provide adequate protection for the patroller; except for a slight but temporary deafness should one of the IEDs be ignited. Don't forget to carry your patrol belt or your back pack with enough dressings and wraps for cuts, lacerations and body parts.

I am finally finishing this first newsletter,   Oops, this just in: Most of the IEDs made, perhaps, from the avalanche cannon explosive rounds may have been detonated.   Fortunately, only the area manager's dog, Rum Keg, was injured and he luckily suffered only a broken tail.   This has been put in a cast and splinted.   The cast, being too heavy to manipulate by "Rummy" has been put in a two wheel cart that is harnessed to him.   Three junior patrollers have been put on a rotating assignment to do dog doo duty.   Their job is to disconnect the cart and hold Rum Keg's tail and the cast up and out of the way when the necessity arises.   Your board of directors will decide appropriate compensation for these young heroes.

Again since we are not sure of the correct count of the missing canon rounds, keep your eyes open and use a ski instructor to break trail in un-swept areas.   Dedicated patrollers are hard to find.   We cannot afford to lose a single one.

I am finally, finally to the end of this newsletter.   The bottom line to all of this is: Be nice and more careful.   (P.S.   Good news: my hang nail is healing nicely, and I have narrowed my search to four likely candidates.)

(Be it understood that these newsletters are pure fiction. They are obviously written in jest.   Everyone knows that patrolling and instructing are important components of ski area activity. There is a healthy friendship and mutual respect between these two groups.   In fact, when patrollers suffer financial hardship, they often become ski instructors.   Patrollers are also aware that customer income and area management are both necessary for the well-being of the slopes and for lift maintenance.   In addition, if the humor described in these essays actually occurred, it would result in the ski area closing down, lawsuits and serious depletion of the party funds.)

5.
Aria's Snow Day
Heather Moser

Freshly fallen flurries painted the ground white.
Aria knew that this meant she might
get to play in the fluffy mounds of snow.
It was time to slip on her boots and go, go, go!
But first Mommy stopped her and explained it is cold.
She must put on the proper attire, she was told.
With every agonizing ounce of patience, she stood
waiting for Mommy to tell her she could
head out into that winter wonderland!
This was her first experience with snow and
she could barely contain herself at all.
A world of excitement bottled in a girl so small.
She eagerly waited in the atrium on the tile
as Mommy opened the closet doors with a smile.
In anticipation, she turned her big brown eyes from her mother
to that of her cute and cuddly baby brother
who, while toddling into the room,
lost his balance on the slick floor. Boom!
She rushed over to console him as he cried out,
fat tears rushed down his cheeks as he began to pout.
Cuddling him in her arms, Aria, at the wise old age of two,
vowed to make him feel better. She knew what to do.
She would make a snowman just for him, one very tall.
From the window, he could watch her do it all!
He smiled at the soothing tone in her voice.
First, she must put on her coat and make a choice
between snow boots bright pink, red, or green.
Donning a rose-colored hat, she was a sight to be seen.
With gloves and snow pants on, she was ready to play!
Outside she headed to spend some of her day!
Baby Jensen stayed cozy in the house and had fun
watching Sissy jump in the snow and tirelessly run.

Someday he would be old enough to participate,
but for now he was content to just watch and wait.
The snowman she built for him was very nice,
but he was anxious to add his own spice.
Yes, next year they will be a perfect pair,
frolicking in the snow and crisp winter air.

6.

Boomerang!
The Gravel Mountain Ski Patrol Newsletter
Earl W. Wolfe

Ski Area Management is very concerned about the uncontrolled use of boomerangs by untrained patrollers at Gravel Mountain. Your Patrol is now forced into a Boomerang refresher every year. The Patrol Boomerang refresher will take place on day four of our annual refresher and we might be forced to take out a loan to purchase some additional half barrels of beer and enough ice to keep them cool. Donations are welcome.

The introduction of boomerangs to patrolling is, to a great extent, a great success. Some novel and newly recommended uses for these devices have been implemented, and are listed below with associated warnings.

1.   Mini boomerangs of knife-grade stainless steel are now available for non-proximal removal of lift tickets from skiers who are causing problems on the slopes. These boomerangs must be kept razor sharp to allow slicing and removing the lift tickets while preventing rips in the ski jackets of the problem skiers. (Sharpness is important for a clean cut and allows a full return of the boomerang to the patroller.) Kudos to Patroller "Twigs" for this chopper of an idea. Mis-thrown boomerangs are a concern (see below) and an "expert" rating is required before anyone is allowed to use these clippers during business hours.

The unexpected demise of two customers came to the attention of area management. These customers always purchased family-season tickets every year, and management is upset with the loss of this budgeted income. We were assessed by management for this loss of revenue and the associated cost of the flowers. Worse, the local constabulary now threatens charges of accidental manslaughter if this ever happens again. Occasional loss of customer body parts resulting from mis-thrown "rangs" continues to be covered by our "no-fault" insurance, but those meanies at the Zeta Insurance Company took the opportunity to increase our premiums by ten percent.   Again, the expert rating is now absolutely necessary because our party fund took a big hit from these forced outlays.

2.	Specially designed high-lift boomerangs are now included with all chairlift evacuation kits to get the evacuation ropes over the lift cable. This bang-up idea is being adopted by many other ski areas. Special care is necessary to properly aim and throw these boomerangs. Unfortunately, eight skiers were injured during an evacuation while we were developing the proper throwing technique; worse: we lost twelve boomerangs this last season during lift evacuations. These boomerangs have to be replaced by money out of our party fund.

3.	Heavy-duty boomerangs are now kept at each lift shack for cutting down skier-made jumps and over-sized moguls. Negatively, four snow machine hoses and various electrical wires were cut by bad throws. Worse, two lift towers are bent at severe angles as a result of careless usage and will have to be repaired. Management is assessing your patrol for costs not covered by insurance - the party fund again.

4.	The Patrol Room now has several boomerangs in the first aid room for bent arm and bent knee splinting. Special thanks to our Winter Emergency Care adviser for providing these. These boomerangs are sterilized and not to be used for back scratching, repairing equipment or trimming toenails.

5.	We had such good luck with specially-weighted and padded "enforcer" boomerangs that they will now be required equipment in every Patroller's back pack. These "enforcers" are to be used only to stop jumpers, racers and line cutters caught in the act.

Enthusiastic patroller boomerang usage has caused management to remonstrate with our patrol director and we must take care to allay those concerns. We are told that we should be embarrassed that Ski School Director Franz Fanszi-Schusser lost three of his curls when one of our Patrollers attempted to use a lift-ticket cutter without proper training.

In another occurrence, our assistant patrol director was ka-bonged by an "enforcer" boomerang thrown on January 23rd. All "enforcers' will now be engraved with the patroller's name and each patroller will be required to account for his "enforcer" at the end of the season.

Please, patrollers, many of you are showing sophomoric irresponsibility and several occurrences proved a need for more maturity plus skill and sensitivity training in the proper application of these most useful devices. Please don't attempt to remove lift tickets from two or more miscreants with a single toss of a mini-rang. One such "flick" missed the targets but deftly cut the manager's coffee cup in half; he wants us to pay the cleaning bill for his brand-new Pierre Cardin silk suit.

Now that our beloved patrol director is recovering at the hospital for people who cannot hold their liquor, our acting patrol director is "front and center." Our APD saw "stars" again on February 1st when an inaccurately thrown boomerang stunningly lifted his Stein Erickson wig. On the bright side, now that our bare-headed APD is "reflecting" on things, management tells us that they are able to decrease night lighting by about 10% when the APD is on the hill, and the sales of sun glasses in the ski shop are up 25%. Your patrol executive committee planned to start a collection to re-cover our APD, but this was quashed soundly by area management. In fact, monetary inducements will be offered by management next year to all patrollers who come to the area "un-locked," waxed and polished. Consider this as a way to replenish our party fund.

A problem occurred on our St. Patrick's Day awards party. Unfortunately, our APD was still disoriented by the boomerang that lifted his "piece" and was hallucinating. This was complicated by his over-indulgence of the cheap beer at the party. He foolishly made a pass at our area manager's daughter. Although Oxalis may appear to be a softie, she does weigh 283 pounds. Her gentle rebuff to our Director's overture knocked him through the large plate glass window on the second floor, over the porch railing and onto the ground below. Fortunately, there were three snowmobiles parked below that partially broke his fall.

We have been able to reduce our manager's complaint from sexual harassment of Oxalis to aggravated attempted suicide. Our AP Director is temporarily incarcerated until he agrees to pay for the repair of the window, the scraped varnish on the railing, the pavement cracked by his fall and the bent handlebars on the snowmobiles. For those of you who were at the ski convention in Acapulco at the time... You might be unable to recognize our lock-less assistant patrol director; photos will be included with our next newsletter. Unfortunately, he is recovering from his injuries at the "resort" run by our local constabulary and the photos had to be retouched to white-out the black stripes on his pajamas and the shadows caused by the steel bars. We will be holding an executive committee meeting tomorrow afternoon to see if we can post his bail with money out of the beer fund. (A volunteer committee rotates visits so that he tans evenly without alternating vertical white and tan stripes on his visage.)

The second item on the a executive committee meeting agenda will be whether our beer fund can afford an upgrade to premium or gourmet beer from the local micro-breweries in the future. Your patrol was terribly embarrassed by the derisive laughter when the other patrols learned that we were drinking that cheap stuff. Donations are welcome.

7.
Bright Scarlet
Joann Grisetti

cardinals cover the sunlit snow
red on white, white on red
move as pieces on a chessboard
across the hill they spread;

into the pines bright scarlet they fly,
chittering, chattering,
voices fill the icy cold air
through frozen branches ring

8.
Brother
Jennifer Koch

In loving memory of Joshua J. Davis
November 1, 1980 – January 19, 2014

He was the kind
to step up as your brother
though you had known.

He was the kind
to teach you of strength
though you had known.

He was the kind
to always look out for me
though I have lost sight of him.

9.

Christmas Dinner at My House
Ruth Sabath Rosenthal

this mother gets to mother her son,
indulge him some. Always, he wants

more. Right now, it's tofu turkey breast.
His girlfriend, sure he'd sampled hers

while she was on the phone, lets him
have it good. His father barks

"Lighten up!" and downs a shot.
Between seconds dished out, con-

versation pushed to the hilt, the son
beseeches the front door be locked,

blinds lowered. He knows, beyond
reason, what lurks in the dark.

It's about then, that this mother hurries
dessert, fills two doggie bags

and buries herself in kitchen chores,
killing time till her brood goes.

10.
Constance
Heather Moser

The end of her senior year of college was approaching far too quickly. It was a time of excitement for most students. The campus was buzzing even though it was rather chilly---it was, after all, still February, and those delving into their final semester were ready for a much-deserved break. Students were already submitting applications for 'real-world' jobs. Others were anxiously awaiting their acceptance letters into graduate school while making themselves ill at the thought of yet another rejection. This final semester was critical for seniors, but Constance feared for her academic future.

Constance had accomplished many things during her years as an undergraduate student, and she was proud of what she had done up to this point. However, her goal from the beginning of her academic career was to graduate with honors: summa cum laude with departmental distinction. "Simple enough!" said her naïve, fresh-out-of-high-school brain. Sure. "How difficult could it be to write a thesis? Just imagine each chapter being a separate six to ten page paper. That can easily be done!"

"HA!" Her now more mature and experienced mind knew better. College was far from simple, and her decision to take more than a full course load every semester to fulfill the requirements of a second major proved to chip away at what little free time she had left in her life. Sure, she had thought, she should add an education minor to the mix: student teaching during her final semester would be fine. Definitely, by that point, she would have her thesis done and ready for defense. She would never allow herself to fall behind with her thesis work. "WRONG."

Instead, Constance, in the middle of lecturing high school students had something constantly gnawing at the back of her thoughts: THESIS DEADLINE...DEFENSE...MAY. There was no escaping it. In order for her to meet the goal that she had set for herself years ago, she needed to find a way to get this thesis done. Somehow. She only had a few weeks to get it finished and ready for defense. In order for this to happen, every moment away from the classroom would need to be spent finishing up research and writing, writing, writing.

Constance was sitting in her advisor's office Tuesday morning. She had taken the morning away from her student teaching assignment to attend university business. This excuse was only permitted twice the entire semester, and she needed to face her advisor. Email could only go so far, and it was beginning to appear as if she was avoiding him and her workload. She nervously gazed through the window to the naked branches of the trees outlining the parking lot below. The tinted office window made it look even drearier than normal. The air seemed suffocating. Her heart was heavy in anticipation of what would undoubtedly be a hint of disappointment in her advisor's voice. He was seated in front of the window, her eyes snapped away from the gloom outside and focused on him, turning the bleak trees into mere shadows behind his head. "Are you going to be able to get this done in time?" Oh, her throat started to constrict at the thought of failure. He surely didn't believe in her abilities any longer. He was so obvious in his tone. She had waited too long to show significant progress, and she knew it. Her own advisor was beginning to question her abilities.

She swallowed her breath and managed to squeak out in a cracking, broken voice, "Do you think I can?"

Sternly, he replied, "If you start now, perhaps. I need to see progress soon, though. Otherwise, we need to reconsider graduating with honors, or we can delay graduation another semester."

Both of those alternatives were absolutely unacceptable to her sense of pride. She had worked so diligently, and that determination to do everything she could above and beyond expectation was what put her in this impossible position in the first place. She could not let that be her downfall, not in her final semester. Thinking to herself for a moment, she hesitantly decided to speak her mind: "I have come too far to let the final hurdle cause me to stumble and fall. I can do this. I will have a finished first chapter by the end of the week, and I will send you another every other day until it is complete."

Her words escaped too quickly for her mind to alert her to the impossibility she had set before herself. She had student teaching commitments to attend to as well. She must have lost her mind, but it was too late now. The pledge had been made, and if graduation was to happen on time with honors, something for which she had worked so hard the last four years, she needed to meet that insane deadline. Besides, she had to remind her advisor that she was worth advising. She needed to re-instill his confidence in her abilities. She was a good student, and both her advisor and she needed to be reminded of that.

Wednesday, after finishing up a day of teaching, Constance retreated to the university library for an all-night excursion on an academic odyssey. She walked into the elevator with a backpack full of books, notes, pencils, snacks, water, and a mini laptop. Entering the elevator she told herself, *Major strides need to be made tonight. Deep breath.* She hit the button for the sixth floor, the floor that, in case her personal arsenal of scholarly research was not enough, contained all sources related to her field. Everything she needed was here.

Ding! The elevator door opened and Constance took another deep breath, this time not for concentration but to enjoy the smell of old books that inhabited this floor. She was at home. She walked to the furthest corner of the floor, beyond a sea of shelves to find a quiet area to set up her workstation. Perfect! A beautiful wooden desk seemed overly inviting. Everything was placed and ready for her to start composing. She sat down in a ragged cloth chair, far too worn to seem appropriate for the pristine desk.

Hours passed. Nothing. She just could not budge that writer's block. She decided to get up and pace the rows of books and clear her mind. She inhaled the ever-comforting smell of books decades old while running her fingers along the smooth spines of the books on the shelves. She hesitated in her favorite section: tales from Ovid, the glorious deeds of Caesar, and the hilarity of Apuleius. This was home. She was at peace. Finally, she decided to head back to the desk. It was early morning, and progress needed to be made. She sat down, tapped the space bar, and again found herself staring at the blinking cursor on the Word document. She buried her head in her hands and wept.

"Ahem." She hesitated her lamentation without lifting her gaze.

"Ahhhhheeem." She clearly heard a voice. No. She had to be too tired.

"Miss...I get the distinct feeling you hear me but are choosing to ignore me."

She turned her gaze to her left while still keeping her forehead resting on her palms. What she saw, however, made her jerk her head upright. She wanted to jump out of the chair but seemed to be frozen.

"Whhhhoo? I mean, what, ARE you?" Her voice was cracking out of fear and concern due to the thing she just observed.

The creature approached her desk, its head tilted slightly to the right. "I am... a friend. I live around here and can sense when someone is in need. You, my dear, appear to be in the market for quality assistance. I am here to help."

"Well, I... I... I don't know what to say. I mean, yes, I need help, b-b-but I didn't ask for help. I didn't pray or summon or make an offering for assistance by the way of... well, by the way of... whatever... you... are. What, exactly, are you? And, how, exactly, can you help me?"

"I can help you because I am gifted. I know all there is to know from the books in this building. I have lived here long enough to read all of them many times through, especially the ones on this floor, as they are my favorite. Don't let the wings and tail fool you; I am a scholar. My short stature also means nothing. Please don't even draw attention to it! That gets old after a while."

With a bit of skepticism, Constance uttered, "Fine. What am I to make of your hooves and horns then?"

Sharply its head snapped upright and its tail flicked the tiled floor, clearly in a state of mild irritation, "Listen, lady. I need to walk sometimes, hence hooves. The horns are from my mother's side. I can do nothing about them."

"Well, certainly, you can understand my hesitancy here due to your appearance and..."

"...don't dwell on trivial matters!!!! Do you need help with your scholastic endeavor? Yes or no?"

"Ye..."

"Well then, I have an offer you cannot refuse. I will write two flawless chapters before daybreak in exchange for... oh, say... that pretty highlighter there!"

"...a highlighter?"

"Take it or leave it. I don't have the time nor the patience for your mockery."

She thought quietly to herself for a moment, pondering the level of her anxiety if her mind was willing to let her see such a horrid creature manifest in front of her eyes. She was sleep deprived. Her subconscious was demanding that she rest for the night. Maybe she should just humor herself and try to analyze this hallucination in the morning.

"Well, two chapters are far beyond what I had hoped to accomplish tonight, and I think it is time for me to take a break anyway, so I will take your deal."

She awoke at daybreak with her head next to the keyboard using her notes as a makeshift pillow. What an odd dream. She hazily tapped the space bar to awaken her computer from its slumber. She could not fathom what filled the screen. Words from top to bottom. Pages and pages of words. She continued to scroll. Thirty pages! Proper formatting, footnotes, page numbers, chapter headings. Two chapter headings, to be exact. But HOW?? Surely she had been dreaming, but she did not recall writing that at all. "Don't dwell!" Echoed in her head.

She began to gingerly pack up her belongings, planning a day of lounging and binge watching her favorite shows. She needed to treat herself after working so diligently throughout the night, even if she had no recollection of it. Just as she began to place her phone in her back pocket of her jeans, the alarm began to sound. School! How could she forget she needed to teach today? Hurriedly, she scooped up her backpack full of supplies and raced toward the elevator. She could not afford to be late to work!

She had intended to take a couple days to recuperate from her odd experience, but her curiosity got the best of her and within a few hours of leaving school, she found herself back at the library sitting in same desk as the night before. She opened the computer, ready to start on the third chapter, only to be met with that taunting blinking cursor again. Two completed chapters were great, but she needed to at least have an outline for the remaining four. Maybe she had set an outlandish goal. She couldn't even remember writing the first two chapters, what did she really expect to happen tonight? "Lightning never strikes twice", her grandmother had always said. This was no exception. Anxiety started to take hold of her mind.

After a couple hours of working herself into a horrible mix of panic and depression, she got up and paced her favorite rows again. Her eyes started to feel heavy, and she realized that she probably didn't get much sleep the night before. Rationalizing why she should just give up and go home, she turned and began to head back to her desk to gather her things. Just as she reached the end of that aisle of books, she heard what sounded like wings flapping nearby.

"Ahem." The impish creature stepped slowly out from the shadowed shelves a few feet away. She jumped back a few feet. This thing seemed familiar, but its gnarled face was too disturbing not to elicit some sort of fear. "Oh! I fell asleep again, didn't I?! I will never get anything completed at this rate. Good thing I am on my way home."

Rolling its eyes and gnashing its teeth in what appeared to be its twisted attempt at a smile, it barked out, "Please! Have more faith in me! I am here to offer you another deal. Two more chapters in exchange for that jeweled bracelet on your wrist."

"But, this bracelet was given to me by a dear friend."

It threw its arms in the air, palms toward the ceiling as if it had heard enough resistance from her, "Superior work on a deadline is not cheap, Constance."

She didn't want to fight with an imaginary friend for a second time. Reluctantly she agreed, so she could find some peace. "Fine."

The bright early morning sunlight woke her this time. A single ray streaming in through the nearby window with the sharpness of a knife. Her head was fuzzy, and it took her a few minutes to realize where she was. Her neck was stiff from having little support and her lower back ached. She really needed to start falling asleep in her own bed, as this was a far cry from a fresh start to her days. Tapping the space bar of her slumbering laptop keyboard, she was flabbergasted to find two new, flawless chapters complete. She started racking her brain, replaying everything she could call to mind from the night before. At first, feeling a mild sense of disgust without understanding why. Retracing her steps, she remembered leaving the school, entering the library, getting to her desk, pacing her favorite row of books, but then her recollection began to fade. She sighed and rested her chin on her right forearm as she leaned on the piles of notes. Something was missing.

Suddenly she realized her bracelet was absent. It must have slipped off of her wrist while she was sleeping. She stood up, scattering her notes all about the desk, lifting books to find nothing. Her hands and knees hit the floor as she examined the underside of her workstation. It was gone. Her favorite bracelet, a silver chain with amethyst beads, was gone. She was devastated. The tears began to well up in her eyes before she could bring herself back to her feet. That bracelet had been given to her by her dear friend, Amanda, before she left to pursue overseas adventures. It was priceless.

Suddenly, as if the fog that had been covering her mind had instantly dissipated, Constance recalled removing the bracelet from her own wrist. She closed her eyes to help focus on the memory. Yes, it was clear. She remembered unfastening the latch, sliding it into her left palm, and handing it to another hand. A disfigured, leathery, and scarred hand with three bony fingers that were tipped with curved claws. Squeezing her eyes more tightly, she moved her mind's eye up from the hand to the thin arm, then a neck, and a face. Oh! What a disturbing face! Its mouth was nearly as wide as its face, but only when it decided to show its small but sharp teeth. The pitch black eyes were deep-set under a brow that stuck out significantly. Massive ears stuck out from the side of the head, flopping a bit and pointing back toward a long tail. They appeared to have large chunks taken out of the edges, almost as if they had been gnawed. Two modest sized black opaque horns that twisted a bit also occupied its head, one near each ear but more centered on the crown of the head. It had ragged wings that seemed to move as a reflection of the creature's mood. It was not very tall at all, and both its stride and feet were reminiscent of Pan. That creature, that thing, whatever it was, had her bracelet. It was also the author of her thesis, though, so although she was horrified, she felt a sense of inexplicable gratitude. If she was losing her mind, this was an interesting character for her brain to create. If this was not a hallucination, she needed to see it again to find out its purpose and, perhaps, get just a little more assistance. She was so close to the end now, and; at this point, she felt like she needed whatever help she could muster. First; however, she needed to report to work. The students would not teach themselves, and; quite frankly, it wouldn't hurt to have a distraction from the vision that had manifested in her brain for a few hours. Getting up off the floor, she packed her belongings and headed to work, taking a mental note to look into the effects of black mold spores on the brain. The library was very old, so she told herself it could be a possibility. The thought of mold contaminating her brain and lungs was only slightly more comforting than the idea that the thing she envisioned was real.

That night she returned, this time hoping she would see the creature she had recalled earlier that morning. Regardless of the reason behind its appearance, the apparition meant work would get done, and if she had the foresight to engage it, maybe she could make sense of what had been happening. Her desires soon dwindled, however, as she set up her workstation and waited. Nothing. Finally, after waiting for quite some time, she gave in to her curiosity and impatience, calling out for the creature.

"I know not your name, but I know your abilities. Please come to assist me, creature of knowledge."

She heard the clicking of hooves at a distance and soon saw the creature pop around the corner of shelving a few rows away. Her mind was clear this time, but upon seeing it, all of her premeditated inquiries of the creature vanished as if its very presence wiped her consciousness clean of her intentions.

"Ah! I see you need more help now, do you? If I am not mistaken, two more chapters tonight will complete this work for you. That, my friend, is going to be of significant cost."

"How significant? It is just two more chapters. You have been doing the same workload all week!"

"Such attitude will not be tolerated! We both know the conclusion is the best part of any story. Without a great conclusion, your arguments will crumble. You need my help? Agree to the price!"

"What is the price?"

"I require all royalties when your thesis gets published."

"No. I wasn't going to publish it. Besides, no one would buy a classics thesis."

"HA! You, clearly, have not read my work! You will publish. They will buy it. I will get the royalties."

She hesitated, but eventually realized that, even if she did entertain him, she could only benefit from the arrangement. No one would read her thesis outside of her defense committee. "Deal!" she exclaimed and everything went black.

When Constance awoke, her thesis was complete. This morning, however, she did not have to struggle to remember the deal made with the creature. Perhaps it was a foolish promise after all, the terms seemed too simple. She started to doubt the bargain. Maybe the creature was more cunning than it looked, but she had no time to worry about that now. Deadlines needed to be met! Straightaway, she walked the flawless work to her professor's office, instantly reinstituting his faith in her abilities. By the end of the week, a defense date was marked on her home calendar, and she had hand delivered copies to her defense committee members for review. Only a few steps stood between her and graduation.

The morning of the defense, Constance arrived in the conference room ahead of her committee, arms full of doughnuts, napkins, and plates. She had premium fresh coffee delivered a few minutes before the defense began because she wanted the experience to be enjoyable for everyone involved. She was proud of the work she was about to defend, but she still had a nagging suspicion that no one would find it even mildly entertaining. In fact, she would completely understand if all of the committee, with the exception of her own advisor, had opted to skim the pages, highlighting random sentences and an occasional footnote in an attempt to give the illusion they had read it cover-to-cover. Either way, she had spent days preparing for the myriad of questions they could ask her. While reviewing her research, it was so odd how much of it naturally came back to her for not having written a bit of the work. It was almost as if she could remember watching the imp type away at her keyboard while she absorbed each letter on the screen as it appeared.

The committee entered right on time, pleasantly surprised by the breakfast waiting for them. She summarized her work and theories, and each member took a turn asking her mildly probing questions, all of which she answered comprehensively and with ease. They seemed genuinely impressed with what they had read. She was dismissed to wait in the hallway, and after a short deliberation, she was called back in the room. Her advisor stood up, congratulated her on a job well done, and delivered the news that she passed her defense. He added that this was the first time that he had seen a work that needed so little revision. Just a few minor adjustments and it would be ready to be submitted to the university! Her committee members all shook her hand in exchange for a smile and words of gratitude from Constance. As they filed out of the room, she was overjoyed. She finally realized that her dream of graduating with honors, a goal she had worked so hard to attain, was finally going to happen.

Upon suggestion from her defense committee, she decided to copyright her work after graduation. She was euphoric when she received a letter in the mail one day, alerting her that her transcript was now a part of the Library of Congress as a result of her copyright efforts. Amazingly, before she could even look into any further steps, a publishing company contacted her via email. In their correspondence, they explained that one of their scouts, who is employed to scour all new arrivals in Washington DC, had been particularly impressed with her thesis. It was due to the scout's suggestion that they examined it and concluded her work would be a valuable asset to their publishing company. It seemed like a dream, but it was so very real. Within a couple months and a few minor edits to make it more appealing for mass audience consumption, it was officially in the hands of the public. By some bizarre occurrence, her work was flying off the shelves, even selling out in some university bookstores! It was a whirlwind of positive activity, and she was elated. Occasionally, however, she would have an abrupt feeling of concern, recalling the look of satisfaction on the creature's face when she made the final deal. Yet, almost within the same breath, she would snap herself out of that fear, saying aloud "Don't dwell!" and moving on to the next task at hand as if nothing ever happened.

Before she realized it, her first royalty check was delivered. She had just begun to tear the end of the envelope when she heard that nearly forgotten voice and the clacking of hooves on her hardwood floor. "Ahem!" Constance whipped around in a state of disbelief, but before she could speak, the familiar creature barked out, "I believe you owe me something."

Deep down, she always knew this was coming, although she had hoped she wouldn't ever have to confront the ugly thing again. In a fit of frustration, she retorted snidely, "You cannot be serious. I really thought you weren't real."

Bowing before her, it smirked, "I am real, indeed. As you see me standing here before you, I am real. I am tangible. See." It snatched the partially opened envelope out of her hand, slicing her index finger in the process. It snickered when Constance winced with pain.

Thoroughly annoyed by the attitude of this snarky little creature, she grabbed back her envelope without hesitation. With her voice elevated, she started toward the creature with full intent of grabbing it by its floppy ears and throwing it out the front door. "This is absurd! I deserve this. I NEED this. I have yet to find employment and student loans need to be paid. You cannot have this."

As she approached, the creature exclaimed in a sense of unease, "We made a deal!"

"There has to be another way," she insisted as she began to reach down toward the creature, now backed up against the wall.

"Perhaps we can work out an alternative deal," it shrieked in fearful anticipation. She stopped, straightening her spine. Tapping its middle claw against its chin. "Yes, if you can guess my name, I will leave you forever. Or, at least until you have another academic endeavor you cannot personally complete. You have three guesses."

Although this sounded like a completely ridiculous trick, the creature seemed genuinely willing to let her keep the money if she just humored it. "How could I even begin to... alright. It is worth a try. You look like a... Charles?"

Flitting its tail with a minor sense of victory, "Ha! No! Wrong sex!"

Slightly embarrassed, although she was not completely sure why, she apologized, "Oh. Forgive me! Polly?"

"HA! Do I look like a parrot?? Ahhh, I can practically smell the money now. Mom sure could use some help."

Mom? She couldn't even imagine what the mother of such a hideous thing would look like. Nevertheless, the familial sentiment did strike a chord with her. "What do you mean your mom could use the help?"

Turning its back to her while sheepishly peering back over its shoulder as if capable of human emotion, it replied: "Not that it is any of your business, but if you must know... my mother suffers from MS and needs funds for a new medicine."

Constance was floored. It was almost as if she was talking to an imp-like version of herself. Her mother was also afflicted by the same life altering disease. "Wow. I didn't know that creatures like you could suffer from illnesses. How odd that my mom is in the same situa.... Wait!" The oxygen rushed out of her lungs, and she was speechless for quite some time, her body motionless with fear. It couldn't be possible. Her head started shaking violently, no, no, no. Her eyes filling with tears, she regained just enough breath to whisper, meekly inquiring, "Is your name... Constance? Are you... me??"

Instantaneously, the imp disappeared as if it had never existed. Her silver bracelet was all that was left on the floor in front of her. Constance was fully engulfed in an epiphany. The apparition... that imp... was her. It all finally made sense. The creature was a physical manifestation of her abilities that came forth when stress was too much for her conscious mind. Her subconscious had taken over in the hours of need, and she succeeded. She had pushed herself beyond what she had ever imagined possible without realizing it. It was scary, and it was frustrating, but her life had been forever changed for the better. Finally enlightened, she had a tugging feeling in her chest that this would not be the last time the imp would make an appearance. If only she could control it. She started to imagine what she could accomplish if she could harness this ability. What other ways could she succeed in this world with that kind of power and determination? Oh, it was overwhelming to think of all the possibilities. Her mind began to echo: *Don't dwell!!*

11.
Falling in My Neck of the Woods
Ruth Sabath Rosenthal

Bird chirp. Coffee perk –
sounds that may fall on deaf ears.
Hard hearts, the loveless.

Today's New York Times,
yesterday's trees. Branches stir.
Petal-fall. Summer.

Tomorrow's paper,
today's news hacked and rehashed.
Verdant leaves brown. Fall.

One November night,
a ghost of a smile crosses
the moon, hails winter.

Trees dig in, boughs tough
it out. I struggle writing
haiku.

12.
First Color
J. P. Christiansen

Where, Sibelius,
are you going
on those galloping string-notes of impatience
into the woods of North,
into the darkness of frigid winter?

What, Sibelius,
are you looking for in the desolate barrenness,
where hidden life in hibernal sleep lies waiting
for Gaia's tilt it to awaken?

Wonder,
the lonely land of notes' despairing gloom
weighed to almost silence in the bitter cold,
slowed to almost stillness by rest imitating death.

Wander, then,
across the field of white
until you find the brave color rising through the flute
as it breaks the cover of melting sorrow.

It is then, Sibelius,
that in the woodwinds' light of sun
I hear the yearning of galloping notes ...
it is then,
when sounds the first color,
I know where you are going.

13.
The First Morning
Tonya Moreno

The house is so quiet this morning
Without you in it
You the last of the four
The loudest to leave
We quake in the wake of your silence.

No more laps to give
Or good morning hugs
No meditation snuggler or
Yoga partner

No more
Struggling to breathe or
Being forced to eat or drink
No more

You made our lives so much fuller
With just your silent presence
And now we are less
Without you.

14.
From The Frozen Void
J. P. Christiansen

Life's weather-imposed interference
crackles and rattles my reception;
winter's winds lends noise to me.

Beneath ice and snow, blowing,
lies I, in patience, waiting for me.

When I'm too much of this world,
and overcome by its comings and goings,
I await the call to still my restless heart.

When I'm too much of this world,
I long for Massenet's 'Meditation from Thais',
so I may see through noise of unforgiving irrelevance,
and Shostakovich's violin-concerto sounds the long, cold
hard winter when I gather strength for the awaited moment
of once again coming alive to the call and its desire,

and when words rise from the frozen void
I know for what I live and endure.

15.
Frozen Flowers
Deborah Guzzi

Tufted white-tops on pale beige, staggered stalks,
the coneflowers crowned dress the perennial bed
leaning precariously against the conical
mushroom shaped birdbath.

Snow, soft and wet wraps the grape arbor like ermine,
making trellises reminiscent of Kanji on a blank page.
Fragile, frozen, flowers hang decoratively,
from frail clematis twining about cedar posts.

Brittle, brown, maple leaves, left behind by autumn;
drag branches draped, as in bridal lace, to the frosted tarp
defying winter to do what fall could not.

Conifers cry under the weighty white down,
their limbs straining not to crack, surrender
snap to attention as the day warms.
The snow plops pleasantly to the ground.
Winter waits patiently as the garden dreams on.

16.
Genevieve
Heather Moser

"You are one of the best up and coming stars, Genevieve!" Zack exclaimed in an attempt to instill just a sliver of confidence into his apprentice. He was an experienced superstar, at least in the realm of magicians, and she was... well... she was a young girl from a small town with an apparent fear of public performance. It was the heart of winter. Snow had snarled traffic for days, but Zack and Genevieve, desperately needing to practice, decided to barricade themselves in the auditorium they had rented with all provisions necessary to ride out the latest winter storm. This winter campout was vital to their mutual success. They were gearing up for a world tour, and the first performance was rapidly approaching. Magical Realms of Wonder was Zack's vision, but he needed a partner to assist and perform independently on occasion.

Genevieve was talented and beautiful. It was purely by chance they had met, when he stopped at a local mom-and-pop diner for a quick bite after his morning run. There she sat in a booth across the aisle. She was a vision and had an infectious smile. A bit of ornery ran through her, he could tell, as she placed a deck of cards on the table, telling her girlfriend to 'pick a card, any card.' He pretended to not notice at the time, but her slight of hand was beyond that of a novice. Her presence was that of a veteran. He saw a diamond in the rough, and he knew he could polish her to perfection. When the girls were finished eating, he walked over and offered to buy their meal, using his flirtatious smile to strike up a conversation. She admitted to being an aspiring magician, and he shared his ideas for their future. The rest was history.

Unfortunately for both of them, her natural abilities did not prohibit her from having stage fright. She was brilliant as an assistant, but her hesitancy to perform independently increased when discussing the final act. She had to hypnotize someone. He had all the faith in the world in her ability, but she swore she knew very little of the art. He sat down into a metal chair placed directly in the center of the stage as she walked in front of him with mild trepidation.

"Let's try one more time. If you can't handle this, we will have to come up with something else to leave the crowd in awe." Genevieve reluctantly dangled the pocket watch from her closed fist. This was the time. She had him exactly where she needed him, and her months-long act of innocence was about to come to fruition. "OK, Zack. Please focus on this golden watch. Follow its movements carefully. Your eyes are heavy. Limbs are relaxing. Feel the weight of your anxieties and concerns melt out of your mind and core, move through your legs, and slide down into the floor. Close your eyes. 3... 2... 1." She stopped the motion of the watch by flipping it in her palm, tucking it away into her dress and smiling to herself. He was in her domain now. "Open your eyes."

Zack blankly gazed around the room for a few seconds, finally resting his eyes on Genevieve standing before him. "Hello, Zack. You are in an auditorium, here as my apprentice. We are rehearsing for our world tour, and I know with sufficient practice, you can rival the greatest magicians. All you need to do is quietly abide by my orders. You will smile at the crowd. Make them feel welcome, but you are NOT the star of the show. You are my handsome assistant, and if you earn it, I will let you have more stage presence. You just aren't quite ready for much more responsibility. Do you understand?" Zack nodded. "Excellent! Now, I need you to sign this paper for me. It is simply stating that you are aware of and agree to your role during this tour. You will be paid appropriately. This is simply a precaution to ensure that you don't get any silly ideas like you are the main attraction or the profits are primarily yours." She snickered in a mixture of satisfaction and mild disbelief as she handed him a pen and he began to sign on the dotted line, handing her the contract when he finished.

It was complete! So many years of practicing the art of magic, perfecting her ability of hypnosis, and learning how to appropriately intertwine innocence with sex appeal finally paid off. She was about to be a star in a business that had slammed so many doors in her face time and again telling her she was pretty enough to be sawed in half but women had no place as a headliner. The tide had just turned, and she had an ironclad contract that could not be contested. Now, to snap him out of this hypnosis successfully so she could begin her ascent to fame.

"Thank you for your signature, Zack. We are going to continue practicing our acts in just a moment. Remember, you are very talented, so talented that you dream on a nightly basis of future achievements. These dreams are your goals that you have set for yourself, nothing more, but I will do everything I can to help you get reach those goals! Now, close your eyes. Three... two... one." She snapped her fingers.

"Wow, Genevieve! That was so refreshing! Let's get back to work! I want to be as successful as you someday, and I am so thankful for the opportunity to perform with you!" As the words escaped his mouth he felt as if he should be mourning some sort of loss. For what he needed to grieve he could not decide, but he felt a hole in his heart as if his life's work had slipped through his fingers. How silly he thought to himself. He needed to get back to work. A novice needs practice, and they were going be touring soon. He really was lucky such a lovely young woman was willing to mentor him.

A few months after that fateful winter campout, as they began their fourth show in Paris, Genevieve had already gained international stardom. Zack proudly handed her the saw as he crawled into his box. Someday he could be the star; he just had to pay his dues.

17.
Happy
Jennifer Koch

In loving memory of Cletus Charles Gonyea
July 29, 1928 – December 10, 2013

The first winter storm in Michigan—
it's cold, it's raging; the elements are warring.
But, I grinned, and I bore it
                 as my father drove.
We'd set off to a funeral, a sad affair
that matched the weather—and
                 certain Michiganders driving skills.

Uncle Clete had returned to Heaven
before the storm that could not rest
a colder chill upon us.
                 Dear Uncle Clete.
He wasn't a true uncle, but a great
uncle who everyone just called uncle—
                 that, and Happy.

Always happy, always the clown—
a genuine clown, with balloon animals
by the bucket loads.
                 Happy Clete the Clown.
As the weather wars against these walls,
here within it is warm, happy—
                 despite the tears as the flag is lifted.

Even though I sit here cold in the back row
and a war of words rages in my mind
a kin to the furry of the cold wave beyond —
                 their religion and mine;
as the tears roll down my cheeks,
a smile rests on my face.
                 Happy.

18.
Holding Winter's Hand
A. J. Huffman

as together we kick the dead
leaves of autumn from the footpaths
still open to transgression.   United
in exhaustion and the frustration of
brittle crunching beneath our feet,
we are determined to construct
a world reborn in soft white.   The glitter
of a cotton-like covering will buffer
our boots, allow them to sink, unsounding,
sneak up with snowballs, rain silent surprise.
A swoosh of a sled or two might rupture
the pristine portrait of a hillside before the sun
comes out.   We linger to watch,
as our fingers slowly separate,
as our frozen foundation begins
to melt away.

19.
Home for the Holidays
A. D. VanKirk

Ghosts assaulted me as I walked into the old house. They appeared in the form of dust and memories. It was difficult to say whether these ghosts were the newest residents of our old, abandoned home or simply the same tired tenants of my mind. My sister stood next to me. She said nothing, something not unusual. It had been years since we were in the same room together. She had moved out to Denver to teach, and I had escaped to Seattle to nestle between mountains and the sea, the perfect place to write and sip the finest coffee I knew.

We had never been close; when we were younger we bickered and fought like cats and dogs. As I grew older, I tried to reconnect with her, but she would have none of it. Eventually, I gave up, and we just left it at that. So, when Summer called to ask if I was heading to our parents' house in Wolverine, Michigan for Christmas, I was quite surprised. I told her that I was. She said that she was planning to fly into Toledo and urged me to do so as well. She wanted to meet so we could go shopping at the mall there, as we did when we were younger. She offered to rent a car so we could explore the city where we grew up, and afterwards head to Mom and Pops'. There were definitely better and less expensive travel arrangements, but I was intrigued by Summer's suggestion and so, agreed to it.

I waited for her at the airport for several hours. Sitting in the uncomfortable chairs with the out-dated red velvet cushions, I pondered why Summer had suggested this peculiar method of travel. It hadn't been the first time I had wondered this, but there, at the threshold to this strange adventure, I questioned her motives amidst the vortex of excitement and confusion. Summer was not the sentimental type, but I wondered if being a teacher had changed her.

She found me and my pool of thoughts and crashed her giant purse into my knee. "Ready to go?" was all she said. We found the car rental station, and as planned, rented a car so we could drive to Wolverine, but stopping at Franklin Park Mall on the way. We walked through the mall we used to frequent when we were younger, but it had all changed. None of the stores were as we remembered, and the whole place had fallen into disrepair. I wanted to throw a penny into the fountain like how I used to when I was a kid. The fountain was gone, and in its place was a kiosk selling sunglasses. I felt as sad as the middle-aged woman manning that kiosk looked. Summer kept quiet about the changes to the mall, that to me, felt like defacements to national monuments. When we began the drive to our parents', the amount of conversation hardly improved. I could not remember a more awkward car ride, which was sad since the one I was sharing the car with was my own sister.

"How are your kids this year?" I asked.

"They're fine."

"I mean, are there any kids that give you a hard time?" I pressed, trying to engage her in some sort of conversation.

"Not really."

"Oh."

As we traveled the highway, Summer flipped on her turn signal and headed toward an exit ramp. I asked her where we were going and if she needed to use the bathroom.

"No. I want to have a look at the old house. I haven't seen it in years. I still have a key; never gave it back to Mom."

It took me a moment before I realized it was the same exit we used to take home whenever we went to Toledo. I had forgotten all about those country roads, and it was like I was seeing it all again for the first time. We passed the spot where I got into a car accident one winter on my way to school. Naturally, my sister pointed it out to me, remarking, "Remember that one, Skid?" She'd revived the old nickname my family bestowed upon me after my Jeep slid over the ice into the car waiting at a stop sign in front of me.

Irritated, I nodded sharply.

We pulled into the driveway. I got out of the car and immediately began to relive my childhood. A thin layer of ice covered the pond in the yard where Summer and I used to swim in the warmer months. In the winter, the place was always gray and dead, resisting the blanket of white we had driven through on our way up. The trees were grim, almost leafless save a few dead ones that clung to the nearly naked branches. The grasses had long since turned brown, and the yard stretched out, quite empty.

Contrary to all that I've said, the house was beautiful and the yard landscaped tastefully, objectively speaking. Despite this, my parents were still trying to sell that house. It had been seven years since they first put it up for sale. They tried lowering the price three times, but it had not done much good. From what Mom has told me, they have nearly closed the deal on it many times, but the new family always backed out.

As Summer and I walked into the house, and the ghosts appeared, neither of us said a word to the other. She stepped further in, brushing the dusty, cranberry-colored wall with her mitten as she walked, leaving a trail as it passed over. I followed her, but diverged from her path and headed toward the old wood-burning stove. Normally, at this time of year, there would have been a fire crackling away, warming the house. Pops was determined to save a few bucks and refused to turn on the heat. The fire was an obsession of his; like the Olympic flame, we were forbidden from letting it go out. There were serious consequences if we did not place more wood on the fire and allowed the flames to die. With the first frost, the fire was started, and the same flames burned until Pops let it go out with the coming of the first thaw. Seeing it brought back memories of our first Christmas spent in that house. We sat by that stove, on the floor because there had been no furniture. We unwrapped the gifts in our coats because the heat was not functioning yet, and we had no logs for the stove on hand. I had hated it, but Mom wanted us to be in that cold house. Not much changed during the years Summer and I lived there.

Summer came to stand by me and gazed at the mantel piece above the stove where pictures of the family used to rest. Now bare, she stared as if she could still see the smiling faces frozen in film and encased in woody prisons. I left her there to climb the steps to my old room; it was eerie seeing it empty. I looked at the carpeting and thought I could still make out the impressions of where the bed had rested for eighteen years. There were cobwebs in the corners, trapping dust and memories, causing me to wonder why the realty company was not keeping the place in better order. Maybe they had given up. It was stuffy in my old room, just as I remember it. Out of habit, I switched on the ceiling fan. A blizzard of dust filled the room and, after my second sneeze, I decided it was better to leave it off.

Sitting cross-legged in the middle of my old room, I looked all around, allowing the ghosts to do their work. I was reminded of the countless times I used to seek sanctuary there while Pops stormed around downstairs drunkenly, smashing plates against the wall or screaming at Mom. I remembered cowering beneath the covers, acting as my own sentinel. I'd wait for the creatures that lurked in my closet to emerge, until I grew too tired in my watch and fell asleep, daring the monsters to do their worst. There were times when I read the Bible, searching for answers I would never find, seeking comfort in pages and words that held no meaning for me. I used to sequester myself in this room and drown in tears and poetic words. It was here where I made my resolve to stop letting the world tell me who I was and to start telling the world who I was going to be.

The walls leaned in around me, as if eagerly waiting to see what I would do next. Once so white in their manufactured purity, the walls had darkened to a shade of ashy gray, bathed in the same dust that coated the rest of the house. In my mind, I dismissed their glares and fended off the ghosts long enough to stand back up. Glancing at my watch, I saw that I had been sitting there for nearly a half hour. I wondered if Summer had been plagued by her own ghosts.

Walking down the steps, I saw Summer huddled over herself, leaning against the stove, as if seeking warmth. As I grew closer, I noticed the tears dripping down her face. Summer never cried; I was always the crybaby. She internalized her emotions, using them to fuel her exercise. To see her cry now was disheartening. If Summer, the stronger of us, was crying, what hope was there for me against the ghosts? There would be no comforting her; it would only make her angry. I knew nothing of her ghosts anyway, or how to protect her from them.

I sat next to her at a reasonable distance, any closer and it would have pissed her off. Without looking at her, I said that I hated this place. She sniffed, "Me too."

Rummaging around in her coat pocket, she took out a lighter and a pack of cigarettes. She lit one up, took a puff, and blew the smoke up at the ceiling. "I didn't know you smoked," I said.

"There's a lot you don't know about me, Eli," she replied.

We sat in silence for a moment. "Can I have a hit off that?" She gave me a look that said she did not believe I smoked and thought I was trying to artificially bond with her in the sappy way I used to try. "There's a lot you don't know about me, Summer," I said with a half-smile.

She took a puff then passed it over to me. I breathed the smoke in deep. The house was as cold as it had always been, but the cinders at the end of that cigarette we shared warmed the place the tiniest bit.

We left in a hurry after that. Summer sped down the driveway, eager to be back on the road that would guide us to the highway. I looked in the rearview mirror and saw wisps of smoke rising from the chimney. It was the last I saw of that house, and I was happy to watch it fade. That place was never a home to Summer or me. Once it was completely out of sight, Summer and I began to talk. We did not stop until we walked through the door of Mom and Pops' place in Wolverine. We were greeted with hugs from Mom, a nod from Pops, and a roaring fireplace.

20.
How That Chunk Of Snow – Haiku
John Fitzpatrick

How that chunk of snow
crowned with sludge of winter grime
refuses to go.

21.
I Am Winter
A. J. Huffman

Vein of frozen white, I am innocent
numbness spreading through insulated limbs,
an involuntary urge to stay indoors.
I am visible
         breath, condensation,
a fleeting trail of exhalation.   I am fingerless
form covering hands, debilitating.   I am packed
balls meant for propulsion, an ambush of giggles.
I am aching
         back shoveling path, two feet
stomping clean in foyer.   I am thawing,
a pitiful puddle, evaporating instantly
in generated heat.

22.
I Never Saw Anyone Actually
Ruth Sabath Rosenthal

wear a sweater my Aunt Minna made. Each Christmas,
we thanked her, praised her, held up whichever one
she handed us. Held it against ourselves, showing off
the argyle crew neck or raglan-sleeve cardigan, too heavy
for the slim framed, too flimsy for the broad. And to boot,

the colors, oh the colors she picked to knit: shades of
off-green and puce, and sale yarn at that. Colorblind
to our skin tones, heedless of our body shapes, she knitted
on and on, her bone needles clicking and clacking their way to
the end of each row of sale yarn, pin-pointing her knack

for growing each garment less and less into what we needed,
wanted. Her efforts, though collectively rewarding her
with love and attention, thwarted any requests for
future sweaters, let alone hats, scarves or gloves;
so she turned to crocheting —

crocheting more sale yarn into a carton-full of four-
inch squares she fabricated into one afghan after another.
What followed that was the last of her creations: neon
pom-pom tassels for tying on luggage, which allowed her
to use up every last bit of leftover yarn in her possession.

To this day, those eye-popping beauties adorn a very select
group of suitcases that ride round airport carousels, sit in
baggage claims, stand among a throng of travelers anywhere,
anytime. And each time I eye one, I smile.

23.
Ice Dreams
Deborah Guzzi

Sherbet has spilt upon the evening sky
in cool shades of raspberry and popsicle blue
creaming the horizon in layers of startled
light for Venus rises and licks the bowl of night.

Tongues of petal pink twirl through the forest
lapping the nonpareils shots off chocolate trees.
Spoon in hand the sweet tart of eve scrapes
the curvaceous hollows and frozen icy dells.

As night fills the empty bowl of sweetened dusk,
Venus joins her Hephaestus their ardor rising.
His fires melt the shots of candied moonlight
and fill the celestial sky with new confections.

24.

Joy

Susanne Sack

Written in the winter of 2003 after the birth of a grandchild and the day after my daughter's birthday.

The smallest of specks, dots, encoded strands join,
    swimmingly, inescapably, spliced.
The beginning: never to return to nothing.
    Forever the sky is split.
    The earth is graced.
    The reverberation of the bell sounds,
    the never before heard tinkle of giggle-joy cry.

Needs, wants, demands, never to be unknown,
    burst in.
Small, helpless, never to be ignored garments
    decorate the floor, walls, doorknobs.
Hours lengthen, time disappears
    never to return, never missed.
Time fills with heart-expanding,
    soul growing, color enhancing,
    twinking music of the spirit.

The body droops. The endurance wanes
The heart expands to near balloon stretch.
The joy scale tips.
When were you never?
We can't remember and never will again.
Welcome to the world, to our hearts,
    to our lives, to our vision of life,
    never again to be unchanged!

25.
Ketchup Katastrophie
The Gravel Mountain Ski Patrol Newsletter
Earl W. Wolfe

The Owner and our Manager called a meeting with our executive committee three days ago. Our Patrol is again severely censured by the "front office." The abuse/misuse of ketchup by some of our patrollers has grown to the point where, in the past two weeks, the media were flown in by helicopters several times to photograph the sites of "major accidents". Unfortunately, with misplaced humor, two or three patrollers have taken up the practice of decorating the dressings of injured skiers with inspired paintings of ketchup, so that even skiers with a slight sprain or a strained muscle, leave the area looking like victims of a shoot-out.

Some of the snow at the area is also becoming an embarrassing pink, and the ski school director has complained to management about the splash of ketchup that appears on the snow whenever a ski instructor falls. The splashes of ketchup that may "magically" appear on the heads of bald-headed skiers do not help with the area's appearance of a disaster site. We received several minor complaints because Rummy, the patrol director's dog, knocked several "ketchuped" skiers down to get at the sauce "on top of old baldies."

Your executive committee believes that the major reason for the management complaint is the cost to the area of the unbudgeted gallons of ketchup and the resulting rolls of paper toweling necessary for clean-up. In addition, the area manager has started to use bleach, oxy-white and hydrogen peroxide to whiten the snow where it has been splashed with ketchup. He demands that the patrol reimburse him for the unbudgeted ketchup, toweling and bleach costs that the area has incurred from ketchup "misuse". This money will have to come out of the party fund.

Junior patrollers: please spend more time helping fallen skiers, especially on the bunny slopes and along the chair lift on and off ramps, and pick up (spilled) loose change to make up the deficit. Fortunately, the chair lift operators have agreed to split proceeds from all monetarily beneficial spills. Improper entering and exiting of the chairs, combined with the skill of the operators at the top and the bottom of the lifts in dumping the customers, has been made into an instructional videotape and is now available to patrols throughout the United States, for a small fee plus shipping and handling. All proceeds, after appropriate division, will go to the party fund.

Bad news: The bleach is dissolving the wax on the bottoms of our skis. On the bright side, the slower skiing speeds have reduced the number of accidents. Bad news: the manager has noticed the reduction in numbers of injured skiers and has notified our patrol that he would like to see a 29.4% reduction in head count.

This undesired result of a few high-jinks has the potential to reach the proportions of a major disaster for our patrol. We have just contacted the ski school and agreed to a truce for the rest of the season. We need an increase in the accident rate to keep our friends on the patrol. The ski instructors agree to instruct beginners on the advanced (black diamond) slopes if the patrol allows ski instructors to continue doing aerials on the bunny slopes (to attract victims/students.) We need the support of everyone for this to be successful.

One last item must be addressed. Ketchup is now on the taboo list. Spider Wontski is looking into disappearing red ink at the local magic and novelty stores. We expect a report soon. An alternative is a bio-degradable red ink that bleaches in sunlight. Is there anyone who can help us with this quest? Vampire blood from Halloween?

26.
Landscape, With Natives
J. P. Christiansen

Goodbye, and please take care of the children.
I'll be home soon, when this journey is over.
...

The landscape of my sought-for language
is shaped like the countries of which it is,
with many islands, surrounded by water.

I sail its ship, and the wind is driving.

I steer to shore, make camp, build fire.

I'm drawn to the light, freely burning
mind above the ennui of conditioning
and territory of having been here before.

This restlessness is my watery wonder,
the knowledge that I'm waiting, there
in a dream which warms, through night's
long journey into lands of realization.

Horizons, visible just beyond questioning,
dare me come along for such unknowns,
where wooden vessels leak 'gainst rowing,
and storms bring hazard by broken plank.

Leaving shore was the hardest of things.

My space is not of matter, air, or place,
but insight which comes to visit, me –
a knowing 'tween neurons, shifting
a kind of love for the humanity, in me.

I make landing on farther shores,
and in this I'll come to know me.

Another winter is approaching my camp.

I draw down this season, of resting
in what are inevitabilities of a must see –
a vow of being, and coming explorers.

The natives look at me with a smile.
They teach me the things of survival.
…

I wonder what you're doing, now.
Are the children in bed, sleeping?

27.
March
Kenneth Henry

I was detained by March, that comely lass,
who, lacking February's eyes and teeth
or April's hopeful heart hid underneath,
demanded ransom paid for all who'd pass.
And lacking beauty of her own, she drew
from each cold victim journeying toward spring
some token pleasantry that she could wring,
adorning winter weary days anew.
The hungry land howled out a mournful plea.
And I, a sorry poet, lacking fare
to sate her hunger, lingered lonely there
beneath the bones of a crabapple tree.

Then perched a crested verse on branches thin...
Spring opened up her arms, and let me in.

28.
Memory Lane Revisited
Jon Moray

I didn't have plans on taking a cross-country trip out west. Many of my colleagues at work suggested I go to the mountains to enjoy the air and do a little skiing. After several weeks of juggling destinations in my head, I decided to put their recommendations to the test. I booked a one-week stay at a four-star hotel right by the mountains. Donning a pair of skis was a little concerning to me, especially since it would be my first time.

Leading up to my vacation, I encountered several disturbing nightmares about being trapped inside of a still body, but being fully cognizant. In my slumber, I am calling out for help but all anyone can see is a fully comatose man on a bed; dead to the world and unresponsive. I have had this nightmare numerous times leading up to my trip. I wondered why I was being haunted by those terrifying nightmares and enlisted advice from friends only to be told that I truly needed to get away.

The morning of the trip, I woke up gasping for air as I battled through another round of my reoccurring nightmare. I had packed the night before and all I needed was a shower and breakfast. The SUV was full of gas and all the necessary maintenance checks were done. I just needed to turn the ignition and go. With a crisp chill in the air and a gleaming sun in my rear view, I pulled out of my neighborhood, stopped at a drive-thru a few miles away and filled up on two breakfast sandwiches and cup of black coffee. I drove twenty miles before turning onto Route 88 for the long haul along the countryside. Route 88 would serve as the long stretch to my destination. A barren road for the first five hundred miles that turned scenic as the hills and mountains neared. I planned to stop over twice to rest and break the repetition of the drive. There were several Sleep-N-Go's along the route that always had availability, so when I felt tired I would pull off the road, check-in and hit the pillow.

I drove at a leisurely pace, respecting the speed limit for the most part as I had heard the local troopers in some of the small pass through towns were ticket hungry. I drove seven hundred miles that day and turned into the motel entrance at about ten o'clock. I had never been that far out west so every mile was an adventure in curiosity. I went to bed with great anticipation of what the next day's travels would bring.

My nightmare was much more magnified that evening as I slept in a tiny room, with flat pillows and a roaring heater. I dreamt of unfamiliar faces peering at me, as I lay frozen on the bed. I often wondered how you can dream of faces you've never met. Were these people fabricated in my imagination or were they people I passed by and only registered in my subconscious?

I woke up the next morning to a loud semi-truck's engine just outside my second story room. I showered, shaved, dressed, and checked out of the motel. The newspaper on the counter called for rain and I noticed I had developed an odd monotone drawl to my voice when I exchanged pleasantries with the front desk clerk. I figured I had caught germs from the room when I slept with my mouth open.

I found another drive-thru along the way and ordered the same thing I ate for breakfast the morning before. I was traveling on Route 88 for about four hours when I came upon a sign that read 'Dugansville – 2 Miles.' I muttered the name of that town to myself repeatedly, wondering where I have heard of it before. The name sounded so familiar. About a half mile later, a billboard advertised 'Grandma's Western Cookery.' The name of that diner rang a familiar tone as well. I was bewildered with intrigue as a low rumbling in my stomach alerted me of my hunger. I decided to turn off at the next exit and follow the signs to Grandma's for a hearty home-style meal.

As I passed certain landmarks, I was overcome with the chilling feeling of experiencing multiple *deja vu* phenomenon. The cowboy statue in front of a small city hall building really tested my memory banks as each turn registered an aura of recognition. I was in this town before. I saw the diner sign past the second light on the right and I parallel parked about fifty feet away. I had developed a distinct nervous tic within the last two weeks that only surfaced when I was flustered, but today my neck was twitching like a chicken.

I reached the diner, which looked like a country home retrofitted for business. I stepped up the creaky wood plank steps and entered through a screened porch. The inside of the establishment was welcoming enough for me to seat myself at a booth by a window facing the street. The bell chime above the door alerted a waitress over to where I sat. I was looking down at a laminated two-sided menu when she approached.

"Good Morning Hon. Welcome to Grandma's. Cup of coffee to start you off?" asked a heavy set, frizzy quaffed, redhead with a peach colored uniform and a ketchup stained apron. As I raised my head to answer, she dropped her pencil upon making eye contact. Her expression was that of a woman who just seen a ghost and about to take its order. She covered her mouth and sat opposite me as I retrieved her pencil from the black and white tiled checkered floor.

"Is there a problem?" I asked, in an attempt to break the eerie silence. My neck began gyrating again as she tried to overcome her frozen stare. My monotone voice caused her to cover her mouth with both hands as if to prevent screaming. She suddenly put her hand to my face and spoke, "Harry? Oh, it can't be. It's impossible."

"Harry?" I asked, squinting, as I tried to read her gaze upon me. "I'm afraid you have me mixed up with someone else."

She removed her hand and cackled, almost at a screeching pitch. "It's you Harry, you've come back. This must be unfinished business or something, that's what it amounts to. I have to call your brother," she exclaimed, continuing her witch-like cackle.

I have heard that annoying laugh in my dreams; many times, over and over again. I studied her face to see if I had seen her in my evenings of unconsciousness. Her face didn't register but that awful sound from her mouth did. She called over an older gentleman wearing faded overalls with a wood handle hammer swaying from the tool loop. His name was "Gentle" Gus, handyman by trade. His gait was slow and purposeless like if he had nothing to do and without a care of doing anything of significance. As he approached the booth, the waitress grabbed his arm and guided him to sit beside her.

"Gus dear, look at him. Look at those marble blue eyes. Look at him twitch. Speak young man, speak, and let your voice be heard to Ol' Gus here," she said, with eyes moving wildly about. His eyebrows lifted as he studied me. He began to rub his grizzled chin and tilted his head as if that would provide a better glimpse.

"Harry, why do you come a haunting this town like this? Boy, you've been dead for fifteen years. You've got no place here scaring up townsfolk. Now git. Ain't nobody afraid of no phantom that's been gone for years," he said, extending a broken pointed index finger.

"You both are off your rockers. My name is Phil Marsten. I am on vacation and I just stopped for a bite to eat. Look, maybe I'll just eat somewhere else."

"Gus, you done upset the man. Get up and go back to your eggs. I'll bring a fill up on your coffee in a minute," she said, trying to diffuse a verbal confrontation between the old man and me.

"Alright, alright. But don't you start any trouble around here. This is a town of peaceful folks that live very simple and plain." He got up and hobbled back to his breakfast. The waitress, whose nametag read Loretta, clutched my hands in hers and massaged my fingers with her thumbs.

"Young man, you may be Phil now, but you were Harry many years ago, before..," she stopped and turned away as tears glossed her eyes.

"Before what?" I asked, perplexed at her change in demeanor. She shook her head not to answer. She took a few moments to gather herself and spoke, "Harry, I mean Phil, I need to introduce you to your brother, I mean someone. Will you stick around long enough to meet him? His name is Lenny Shogant."

This time my eyes widened at hearing the man's name. That name, that last name, Shogant, echoed throughout my nightmares. I began to get a supernatural feeling about me that I could not explain. This town, Loretta's laugh, that name; everything was beginning to feel like home. I entertained the notion that maybe I was once an inhabitant of this town in another time. I shook off the idea and answered Loretta, "I'll stay long enough to eat my meal and fill my gas tank."

Loretta bounced out of the booth and rushed to the pay telephone by the back exit, adjacent to the restrooms. She was buying time because she hadn't even taken my order yet. I watched as she frantically tapped on the side of the Plexiglas privacy divider, awaiting an answer on the other end. Her hand moved over the phone in an attempt to shield her shrieking voice. Three minutes had elapsed when she returned to the booth to finally take my order. I ordered a cheeseburger, fries and a diet Coke. Loretta shuffled to the kitchen and got the cook cracking with the order. She hurried back and again helped herself to the booth seat opposite me.

"I hope you don't mind but I called Lenny, Harry's brother. He just has to meet you. You are a spitting image of Harry. Hon, he was a handsome devil before the accident," she expressed, her light brown eyes sparkling.

"What about the accident?"

"Hon, he was completely paralyzed, couldn't move a bone in his whole body. The doctors told the family there was no brain activity but his poor mother, God bless her heart, held out hope for as long as she could until she ran out of resources to keep them from pulling the plug. They convinced her it was for the best to end his struggle. She's been in agony ever since, poor, poor woman." A voice came from the kitchen summoning to her that my order was ready. While she retrieved my lunch I had a hard time trying to compute the new information she had given me. Was I dreaming Harry's agony? He was tormented in his shell of flesh; I know that from my nightmares. She placed the plate in front of me and almost spilled the soda as she clumsily slammed the plastic cup on the table.

"I'll leave you to your meal. Take your time and enjoy it, hon."

I nodded and dug in. The burger was undercooked but edible, while the fries tasted bland even with a generous amount of salt. I was hungry enough to finish the plate despite the lack of taste. I gulped the soda and motioned Loretta over for the bill. As I got her attention, an older man about the same age as Gus entered the diner. I immediately recognized him as one of the two people I saw looking down at me in my nightmares. It was Lenny, Harry's older brother. He saw me and stopped in his tracks at my appearance. He was dressed like Gus without the hammer loop, and he walked with purpose. His faded blue denim shirt was rolled up above the elbows; a telltale sign of how deep in toil he was. His demeanor was a cross between disbelief and anticipation for some answers. He took a deep breath and approached me. His eyes focused on mine for a moment and then traveled slowly down my seated frame. He sat and tilted his head just like Gus as I resumed my twitching. Silence dominated for several seconds until Loretta, in all her quirkiness, broke the calm with the awful echoes from her vocal chords.

"Lenny, this is Phil Marsten from back east. You can certainly see why I called you down here. Phil, this is Lenny Shogant, Harry's brother."

Lenny extended his hand across the table and I shook, noticing the roughness of his calloused fingers on my palm. He focused on each one of my eyes, alternating between each one as if he were taking a reflex test.

"People around here believe me to be your brother, reincarnated. What do you think of that?" I asked, in an attempt at some conversation. He didn't answer. His focus was locked on my appearance; he probably didn't hear the question.

"I have to admit this town is eerily familiar to me even though before today, I never knew this place existed."
My monotone broke his trance as he finally spoke, "Huh, what was that?"

I was about to repeat when he made a comment about my speech impediment. "You look, act and sound just like my brother. You say this place looks familiar, yet you've never been here? Your neck... with all that moving, we used to call you the human Pez dispenser. Do you have thoughts like my brother?"

"I have had dreams that might've lent a feeling as to what your brother went through in his comatose state. In my dreams, your brother was aware of his surroundings even though he couldn't express it to anyone."

"You've had those kind of dreams?"

"Yes, ever since I booked my skiing trip to the mountains I have had these awful nightmares. It was horrible what your brother went through."

Lenny sat back and hunched down in the booth as his shifty eyes told the story of a man that didn't believe in the supernatural but still could not ignore the testimony I was giving. He paused a few moments as if he was trying to mentally piece together the next question he wanted to ask. Finally he spoke, "Going through those nightmares... was pulling the plug the right thing?"

I paused to gather my thoughts when he just waved away any attempt I could make at an answer. I glanced at the bill and reached in my back pocket for my wallet. I removed a ten-dollar bill, three ones, and got up to leave.

Lenny grabbed my arm. "I want you to take a walk with me through the old neighborhood. Will you do that for me? Will you walk with me?"

"I really have to go. I'm already behind schedule," I answered, as he drew his hand away. He shrugged at Loretta for assistance but "The Cackler" surprisingly remained mum. His disappointment showed as he sat searching for words. I gave Loretta the cash and had her keep the change, which was about twenty percent. I nodded at Lenny and exited the diner.

I hooked a left and walked towards my vehicle when I noticed an older hunter green pickup truck parked in front of my truck. The truck struck an instant memory of me driving that same vehicle. I distinctly recalled a bumper sticker that read "Handyman in a Handy Land." I rushed to the back of the truck and there it was, faded and mud stained, but still somewhat legible.

Lenny caught me looking at the vehicle, which belonged to him. The sight of this truck and the effect it had on my memory convinced me to take Lenny up on his offer.

"Why don't we go for that walk, Lenny? I'll call the hotel and inform them I'll be a late arrival."

We walked side by side as Lenny acted as a tour guide, pointing out landmarks and certain places where Harry did something memorable. Most of what I saw I didn't recollect, probably because it had been fifteen years since Harry was alive here. I did recall the rusted fire hydrant that I was told I ran over just after I had gotten my license. Lenny pointed out the tire marks I had left before I jumped the curb. He laughed at how the marks were still visible after all the time that had passed.

"Lenny, how many miles do you have on your truck?" I asked.

"Around three hundred and seventy five thousand. It survived your accident. I never did replace the bumper. That truck is my livelihood. It is the most recognized vehicle in this town and because of its reliability, I am the towns' most respected handyman."

"What about Gentle Gus?"

"Gentle Gus has had a grudge against me since Harry's accident. He always thought I stole his business out of pity because you were comatose and people thought I needed the business more than him. That's Gus for you. The truth is he's lazy and unreliable. He'll blame everyone but himself."

"That explained the cold reception I got when I met him at the diner."

"Don't pay him no mind." We continued our ambling as I recalled a few street signs. I stopped in my tracks as we came to the intersection of Main and Franklin.

I peered over to the left to see a row of old cracker style houses across the street.

"Twenty-three Franklin Avenue," I muttered, as I saw the house where I recalled a night on the front porch swing, waiting for Lenny to come home from a long day of toil.

"You remember?"

"I dreamt all this," I said, as I led the way to the old but cared for house with a wraparound porch. I was the first to step up onto the porch and quickly went for the swing. I swung and looked out at the scene that my subconscious recreated in my nightmares. Lenny went inside while I took in the cool country air with exhaled pleasure. He returned with what looked like a photo album. He sat beside me as I continued the rhythm of the swing. He opened up the album and narrated each picture and its significance. They were in chronological order and not one of them affected me until he got to pictures of us as young men. There were some nice pictures of us by the truck and even pictures taken of the damage I had done to it. He turned the page and I instantly recognized Harry's mother pictured with Harry, arm-in-arm. I was taken aback at her striking features, as she was the woman I saw in my comatose state in the hospital room beside Lenny.

I stopped him from turning the page as I choked up at the love on her face in that picture. "Lenny, where is she? Where is your Mom?"

Lenny straightened up and stopped the motion of the swing. He was one that thought about what he would say before he would say it. "I am afraid she is bedridden in a nursing home. She's been there for the last five years. She has never been the same since her decision to end Harry's life. I visit with her every day. God bless her, you can tell she is dying inside but still puts on a pleasant demeanor every time I see her."

"Lenny, do you think I should see her? I don't want to shock her in her weakened state, but I feel it is something I must do. Maybe it is fate that I see her."

"I was thinking the same thing. I don't know how she'd react, but I think it's worth a try. She's on the other side of town. Wait here, I'll go get the truck." He jumped off the swing and hurried around the corner out of sight as I continued to look at the album. As I was nearing the end, I came upon a picture of Harry in his coma. I saw the non-existent expression and the nothingness in his eyes. I imagined the sorrow his mom went through and brushed away tears as Lenny pulled up.

I hopped off the swing and opened the heavy creaking passenger door. I got in and recognized the cold metal odor of the vehicle. It rattled and the engine was loud but it got us where we needed to go. "Drive easy, don't speed and you can drive a vehicle for as long as I drove this one. That's what I always say."

We got to the five-story, brick exterior, nursing home in fifteen minutes. We checked in at the security desk and took the elevator to the third floor. We approached a reception desk and the on-call nurse quickly recognized Lenny. I overheard her tell him his mother had very little to eat for breakfast and she didn't want to participate in any of the days' activities. He told her he we would only stay a few minutes. We went from the desk down a long corridor with numbers on the wall signifying how many feet you were from the elevators. We got to room 307 and I followed Lenny in. I stayed in the background as he greeted her with a hug and a kiss. He helped her sit up while adjusting her pillows.

"Mom, there is someone here I want you to see, is that alright?" She nodded slightly as Lenny motioned me forward. As I got closer, her half shut eyes widened at my sight. She pointed at me and looked at Lenny for an explanation. She began to mumble something, but was inaudible to both of us. I was now at the bed on her left side as she reached for me.

"My, my son," she whispered, and began to sob. I drew closer and let my momentum bring me cheek to cheek with her. I could feel her tears on the side of my face as I reached around to embrace her. We were locked for several teary moments. I finally broke the embrace as I began to do my involuntary chicken impression.

"There goes the human Pez dispenser," Lenny said, rolling his eyes and shaking his head.

"Mom," I said, naturally, not thinking for a moment that she wasn't. "Mom, I just want you to know that I love you very much and you made the right decision. You freed me from agony," I struggled to say, as tears beaded my flush cheeks. We embraced again and drenched each other's clothes with the waterworks. A voice from the door broke our embrace as the nurse informed us our intrusion was encroaching on Mom's medication and nap schedule. Lenny and I gave her one last hug before we exited. She managed a smile through her soaked face as I turned back and waved.

We walked toward the elevator as Lenny uttered, "I think it was good idea for her to see you. You probably gave her some piece of mind. Thank you."

"I feel the same way. I think she needed to hear it from me."

We took the elevator down, exited the building and headed to his truck. While driving back I asked, "What caused Harry's accident?"

"He was going out west just like you. I offered to let him drive this truck but he scoffed at the idea, saying he would rent a sports car that would get him there in no time. He liked to drive fast. Anyway, when he was close to his destination, an avalanche engulfed Route 88 and he was thrust off the road and down a hill a hundred feet down. I believe if he had taken my truck he would've missed it altogether but I am speculating of course."

"Of course. I understand," I said, pondering the eerie coincidence of my trip out west on the same road. We got to the diner where my truck was parked and we bid our adieus with a firm handshake. He waved as his truck sputtered away and I got into my vehicle to continue my journey.

I had a six-hour drive ahead of me and I took the speed easy. I was on the road for four hours when all traffic stopped. Drivers were out of their vehicles conversing with each other. I got out of my truck to ascertain the nature of the traffic snarl. A motorist explained there had been an avalanche nine miles up the road that closed down Route 88. It had happened about two hours ago. Several casualties had been reported and an estimated fifty cars were affected by the disaster. After several cell phone inquiries about hotel lodging in the area, I turned around on the median and found a resort hotel at the next exit. It was a scaled down resort compared to the one I had booked but it had a lot of the same amenities, only at a smaller scale. I decided to stay there for the duration of my trip since it did have a hill that was a so-called mountain with skiing capabilities. As I laid my head down for the evening I stared out my window on the fourth floor with the neon resort sign blinking through. I reflected on the days' events and it dawned on me that my stopover in Dugansville might've saved my life. I mentally calculated that I would've been in the vicinity at the time of the avalanche. Fate has a way of happening that way, even if it meant me reliving someone else's life in my dreams.

I enjoyed the week I spent at the resort with the miniature mountain. Heck, I wouldn't have tried to brave the slopes on the bigger mountains anyway. I let myself go with my grooming and had grown a mini beard. The twitching went away and my voice was no longer monotone. I felt like me again, before the nightmares. I haven't had any more nightmares about Harry.

I packed up the truck, relaxed, but disappointed at the finality of my vacation. I checked out and revved up the Explorer to go back home. I planned to drive ten hours that day and check into a hotel about one hundred miles east of Dugansville. The drive was a smooth as could be. I was about five miles from the Dugansville exit when I saw Lenny and his truck, with the hood up on the side of the road. I pulled off the road and pulled up behind the truck. I got out and called to Lenny.

"Lenny. It's good to see you again. Having trouble with the truck?"

"Do I know you?" he said, perplexed. "I appreciate you pulling over but I don't believe we've met before."

"Lenny, it's me, Phil Marsten. We met a week ago. Don't you recognize me? You believed me to be the reincarnation of Harry, your brother."

"You are not the Phil Marsten I met. Heck, Harry never could grow facial hair. Your neck doesn't twitch and you don't have a problem with your speech. Your eyes are light blue. Harry's was deep blue. Now, I don't know who you are but you are not the guy who helped my mom go to her resting place in peace, God bless her soul."

I stood shocked at his lack of recognition; however, I did lose a lot of the attributes that made him believe I was Harry. I was more shocked at the news of his mother passing. "You mom died? When? If you don't mind me asking."

"She died a few days after the visit from Phil. I believe she needed him to see her before she could let go of her life. She was just strong enough to hold on so he could put her at ease. I was on my way home from the funeral when my truck just quit on me."

"Maybe I can help. What do you think the problem is?"

"Well, I pulled over to answer my cell. I don't like to talk on it while driving. I cut off the ignition so I can hear over the engine and when I tried to fire it back up, it wouldn't turn over. It either needs a jump or the starter is stuck."

"Do you have cables?" I asked.

He reached over into the bed of the truck and pulled out the cables. I went to my truck to pull up beside him. Lenny hooked it up and after a few tries, it fired up.

"Thanks. I've been thinking about retiring this old vehicle. Do you know how many miles are on it? Take a guess."

"I'd say about three hundred and seventy five thousand."

"How'd you guess?" he asked, surprised. "Anyway, thanks for your help. You are a lifesaver."

"Lenny, it is you who is the lifesaver. Have a great evening and keep doing what you do best in Dugansville."

"Come again?" he asked, skeptically, at how I knew so much about him.

"Never mind. Take care," I said, and turned back to my truck. I shut the hood and waved as I got into my vehicle. He did the same. I waited for him to pull out onto the road as my headlights shone a light on that faded, muddy, bumper sticker.

29.
Moscow Snow
Mark Hudson

Winter isn't something that Russians hate,
they might just bundle up and ice-skate.
Moscow is not everybody's ideal vacation,
but the "cold war" is no longer a classification.
Sidewalks are crowded as snow comes falling,
and in the snow Russian children are crawling.
People bundle up in big mink coats,
they're up in the mountains with hordes of goats.
A statue of Dostoyevsky stands still,
Russian children climb up an ice hill.
You can take a walk along the Red Square
or wear a winter coat made out of a bear.
Many Russians go to the ice rink,
and wintertime Vodka is what Russians drink.
Some make sculptures out of the ice,
you can pay several rubles as part of your price.
Russians are freezing when winter arrives,
and not everybody always survives.
In America, we're the ultimate complainers,
but in Russia, they might be a little bit saner.
Used to the cold, they accept growing old,
and sit around fireplaces, with fairytales told!

30.
Omnia
Yasmin Khan

The power of light can ignite
Dispel darkness, a token of sight
The prism of perception
Knowledge of comprehension.

Evidence of Almighty's might
Existence of energy burns bright
Extolling the perfections
Of universe, heavens reflections.

Light is pristine, infinite
Outruns sound, lightsome flight
Planet's sparkling effulgence
Sky indulges the opulence.

Religion of goodness upholds
When light of faith, a soul holds.

31.

On Her Porch
Ruth Sabath Rosenthal

after Yeats' "Girl's Song"

She rocks after dinner.
Flurries of stardust sprinkle her
sterling. Inside, the dog, snug
on the still-warm Eames,

shudders with dream, and in the tub,
her prince of a husband soaks,
swirls of pipe smoke
crowning his damp, curly mane.

She rocks and nostalgia reigns
over night beneath moonlight.
Breathless, alit with old flame,
she hastens back

inside and is struck by the sight
of his majesty's limp curls,
white — not that bewitching black
in the locket of this once starry-eyed girl.

32.
Phantasms
Joann Grisetti

a weary sadness
weighs down my breath
yet leaves the feeling
of incompleteness
as snowflakes
weigh down spring
a phantasm
of sparkling cold

what is sadness?
what is a snowflake?
both have little substance
cold and weightless
both melt away
when faced with sunlight
both enter the world
after the New Year

33.
Retrogation
Yasmin Khan

My being is broken and fragmented
Into a thousand conscious pieces.
Each breathing its own troubled breath.
Gasping on inadequate oxygen,
Given to it by the fragmented whole.
My shrink may call it a nervous breakdown.
But for me it is a depression,
Of the highest, of the deepest
Whose roots know not the whole
Feel not the whole.
The thousand grey cells vibrate
In its own individual frequency
The buzz is a pandemonium
No synchronicity in its movement
Thought processes of a hundred different reactions.
Thus a hundred numerous equations
That cannot be equated to an ultimate reason
Floundering, groping for a rational return.

34.
Revelation
K. W. DeWess

Cannibal Woman was sneaking through the woods again. Her crooked parts and hair of snakes glided through shrouds of gusting snow. Jodadoh'gowah sensed her presence and he could only grit his teeth.

She smiled at his distress, flicking tentacles of frigid air at his deerskin capote, nipping at tiny passages along sinew threads to squirm around hollow hairs and chill the young man's soul. His uncles had warned Jodadoh'gowah of Cannibal Woman and the agony of a stomach feeding on itself.

He tucked his fists under his armpits to tap reservoirs of warmth and screamed through the icy gusts of air cutting at his face, "Cannibal Woman, forget the young and old! Attack me, a Cayuga warrior! Show me your skill!"

The warrior's eyes seemed too large for their gaunt sockets, but they were alert and searched for a careless movement that would betray the hag's position.

Like a screeching owl that waited for a mouse to renew its snooping, Cannibal Woman refused his baiting. She used the pale light of the moon filtering through snow to hide within the tortured limbs of a witch hazel tree, as if it were the essence of death. Time was her advantage.

The Mischievous One had sent the North Wind roaring across the ridge crests to summon demons to aid Cannibal Woman. The specters were birthed from cold rocks and the lifeless hulks of trees whose bark was shed long ago, to squeal and wail down the hollows, to whip dull red tips of frozen branches against Jodadoh'gowah's head.

The winter's hoard of snow blanketed streams and plants, its depth reaching a tall man's stomach, interlaced with ice layers formed after the season's heaviest snowfalls. Snow walkers collapsed the crusts with cracking noises that echoed through bleak hollows and warned creatures of a predator's approach. Hunters came back with empty hands. Next year's Sustainers' seeds, the newest tannings, the clan's dogs, and even curious mice were all gone. Only the bark skin of the longhouse and embers of the lodge fire-pits offered protection from the cruel winter's indifference.

The world was in mourning.

Jodadoh'gowah's eyes closed, heavy from pursuing Cannibal Woman through the storm, and his thoughts returned to the family's older mothers. They were inside the lodge brooding over whispered horrors of survival and it terrified him. He prayed to the Creator that the snow pelting his face might dampen the dread that was smoldering within his heart.

"Great Bass." It was a weak voice, from his wife, Neoge'deseno'sgwa. She had exited the lodge. "Our aunts have decided." Her voice ebbed to a whisper. "Forgive them."

The sounds were vapor leaving her lips, crawling into Jodadoh'gowah's ears, dredging raw emotions from the depths of his being. He wanted to scream and run away from the fear, but he was a warrior and must suppress the feeling of his heart being torn from his chest.

Their daughter was the clan's youngest, only eight moons old. It would be her first duty to the clan in this world, to be taken from her mother's breast by the elder women in a desperate attempt to insure others' survival. Neoge'deseno'sgwa was the strength of the clan's bloodline and if she perished, the infant would die without her. If the mother survived, the infant's spirit could return to the womb to be reborn. Life would continue.

Jodadoh'gowah looked away to hide the torment in his face. Neoge'deseno'sgwa pressed her body against his back and wrapped thin arms around his boney chest. She was frail, shuddering, and he turned to embrace and warm her with his body. Her face buried in his chest; her thick black hair pressed against his chin. He caressed her head as lifeless flakes of snow melted on the tears streaming from his eyes.

Their infant would be taken under the morrow's winter sun. The elder women would comfort the baby, melting snow in their mouths as a substitute for Neoge'deseno'sgwa's precious breast milk. Water would not be enough and their daughter would die. Cannibal Woman would gain another victim.

Neoge'deseno'sgwa drooped into her husband's arms and he carried her through the lodge door to their side of the hearth and onto their soft bear mattress. After crying most of the day, the infant daughter was asleep in a tiny fur-wrapped ball across the fire-pit from them, snuggled between two of their aunts.

Jodadoh'gowah lay on his side, hugging his wife while pulling a deerskin coverlet over them. Its insulating hairs nuzzled them and preserved their warmth, fending off the evil spirits throwing themselves against the longhouse. But hunger gnawed at his every nerve. He prayed for sleep to conserve his strength and to escape the wretched aching, yet his mind would not rest.

There were questions that confounded Jodadoh'gowah's beliefs. "How could Cannibal Woman infect his elders, blinding their ideals, deceiving them to commit the unthinkable? How could the Creator allow his daughter to die? Was it my failure to know the will of the Creator, or had the Creator deserted me?"

Echoing in his mind was the oath he had recited on the day of transformation from his youth into the Cayuga warrior brotherhood, two winters before he married into his wife's Bear

Clan. "I am Great Bass, a son nurtured by the Damp Earth People. We are His greatest hunters and preservers of the Creator's world." The word 'preservers' faded from Jodadoh'gowah's world like withering echoes in a dark cavern, as rumpling layers of smoke drifted into his weariness to steal the direction of his thoughts. Glimpses came of his shriveled daughter with her eyes glazing over in the finality of death. He watched for her spirit to return to the Creator where it could be reborn, but could find neither its aura, nor its trace. He looked in vain to the tiny crevasses where the lodge's elm bark slabs imbedded into yellowish globs of ice that seemed to burgeon from the ground and he prayed that Cannibal Woman had not found her. And then there was a swooshing in the air. He turned to see Cannibal Woman flitting around the clan's older women, her ghastly visage hovering by their ears one-by-one.

"Eat her!" the hag said.

Jodadoh'gowah struggled to scare off Cannibal Woman, but his tongue would not shape words. His body had become inanimate, a frozen existence in a barren land while his daughter's vital spark flickered away into the storm.

Awareness slipped away and he crossed the threshold to his sub-conscious. He began to dream.

****

I escape my body and hover above the misery. I float to the lodge door and see demons emerge from decaying stumps in the forest. Their mouths open wide and saliva drips from their blood-stained fangs.

The demons swirl to ready an attack. I smell the decay of their victims and feel the heat of their breath. They will shred my body into the smallest pieces and devour me, my soul never to be whole. Pain and eternal loneliness will be my reward for failing to recognize the Creator's path.   I turn and hide in the smallest cranny of the lodge.

And then in the midst of my terror, I hear a reassuring voice.

"Great Bass! You are My child's hunter!"

I feel the demons flee and my spirit lightens.   I slip through the lodge smoke hole to join a gentle breeze and swirl through blue, pleasant air.   Free from laws of the earthly world, I glide for a time with no meaning, until a modest force pulls me towards a mound of snow in the valley stretching beyond our lodge.

I see a tilted hemlock spreading its arms to protect an animal's ice lodge.   Dark green needles glisten in sharp contrast to the white and gray valley.   Near the hemlock is a great spring with sparkling clear water bubbling from its center to freeze into brilliant thin sheets of ice that gild the surrounding edges.

My spirit pierces into the mound and sees woven leaves supporting brilliant sparkles of snow crystals.

From within the beautiful crystals materializes the image of a beast sleeping. I slip into the icy home's interior and around the motionless creature, before returning through a musky odor and the promise of fragile summer blooms.

Hope seizes my spirit!

I rise through the air and bank in the high currents like the hawk catching a valley's summer draft to lift high above the Allegheny Front's tallest chestnut tree.   My joy soars on the rising and falling channels of air.

Without warning, the trough of rising air that whisked me from my lodge loses its buoyancy. The blue air fades to mingle with hiding places of the forest and become the gray haze of a winter's twilight.

****

Jodadoh'gowah's spirit was hurled back into the confines of his subconscious and settled in his stomach, shooting flames through the winding passages of his bowels. The pain woke him. The real world was quiet. No wind ripping at the slabs of elm bark to penetrate the lodge's skin. No crackles spit from the fire pit's glowing coals. Jodadoh'gowah was alert. He knew the place of his dreamtime. It was near.

He slipped from under the deer blanket and like the wisp of a ghost, crept to the lodge door and peered out through the faint rays of the morning sun shining across the valley. At the hollow's distant edge was the crippled hemlock of his dream. He put on his outer garments and strapped snow walkers to his elk-skin boots. He would break the family's rule against crossing deep snow alone because it was the path given by the Holder of the Heavens to his dream spirit.

Jodadoh'gowah tramped into the frozen basin, his aching eased by patches of blue attacking winter's gray sky. In the early sun, the lurching hemlock's green needles glistened from afar, helping lift each step, beckoning him onward.

Black-capped chickadees flew to a nearby arrow-wood bush and chortled to him, "Be strong of faith! Be strong of faith!" Jodadoh'gowah felt the Creator's vigor pulse through his body.

He traversed the marsh-filled valley, toiling through hawthorn thickets and walls of rushes, over frozen water, finally to the crippled tree, and crawled on top of the mound beneath it. He saw ice sparkling along the edges of a vibrant spring nearby and its energy filled him.   He dug into the mound's tangled mass of mountain laurel with his mittened hands scooping out the snow. He cut through tough, interlocking branches with his knife in one hand, shoveling snow and debris with the other.   He dug and cut until after what seemed to be an eternity, he broke through an ice liner into a black, warm hole.

A dank stench stunned Jodadoh'gowah and he fell backwards, his lungs gasping for clear air.   He looked up from the snow dome and saw Cannibal Woman scowling in the upper branches of the hemlock.

He prayed to the Creator and she vanished, and he heard a whimper, like that of a young child afraid of a new noise.   At first he thought it was Cannibal Woman, but then there was another... and another, from deep within the hole he had hacked out of the snow mound.

His mind filled with the dream's vision, a shadow within the ice.

Rolling to his side he peered into the breach, along a path illuminated by rays of the sun.   In the depths of the den were two bear cubs cowering against their mother, tiny squeals of surprise and fear announcing their first experience with the outside world. They burrowed their heads deep into her enveloping expanse of stomach.

Removing his mittens and holding a deep breath, Jodadoh'gowah leaned into the hole, grabbed the hind feet of the closest cub and dragged it out.   It was larger than a full-grown groundhog and despite its youth, kicked, bit, and punched to free itself from his grip.   Yet its mother slept.

The cries and the kicking ceased as Jodadoh'gowah wedged the cub's head into the snow dome with his right knee and unsheathed his knife. He prayed to the Creator to thank the cub's spirit before slitting its throat. With shaking hands he lifted the cub to slurp the pulsing warm blood. Salty thick fluid rushed to his stomach and it began rolling like young otters playing in a pool of water. He dropped the cub and pulled knees against his chin to fight the urge to retch.

After a short time, the air was no longer cold.

Jodadoh'gowah bound the cub with basswood cord to his chest and began to retrace his steps across the valley and up the hill to the lodge.

Near the crest his intestinal pain became so acute that he doubled over into the snow. The snow walkers had kept him on top of the many layers of snowfalls, but in falling, he sliced through those layers, and when he tried to lift his body, arms plunged through the snow to their pits. He could not move.

Cannibal Woman sent crows to surround him and in their raucous style, they cawed, "Eat him! Eat him! Eat him!"

Jodadoh'gowah was too tired to lift his head and he could only stare at the crows. A wondrous sense of ease allowed his body to become one with the snow. Light dimmed.

****

Gentle hands massaged away the prickliness of a thousand hawthorn spines. A warm fatty broth touched Jodadoh'gowah's lips and he swallowed it.

"He awakes," said a voice cradling his head.

Jodadoh'gowah wondered if it were his wife or a demon speaking. He looked through the tiniest of slits for a glimpse of the face above him.

"Do you like the taste?" she asked.

It was Cannibal Woman! Jodadoh'gowah howled and tried to choke the witch. But arms restrained him. His eyes opened wide. Outside the lodge door he could see the sun halfway through its journey across a brilliant blue sky. His family was smiling.

"Your faith saved us," Neoge'deseno'sgwa' said.

He looked from his wife's lap and saw their daughter, vibrant, suckling. Jodadoh'gowah sat up.

His wife's father took a pinch of sacred tobacco from his pouch and sprinkled it into the fire. As the tobacco flakes caught fire and began rising in the smoke, the father took the cub's skin and held it above his head. He sang a prayer of praise to the Creator and thanked the cub's spirit for its bravery in saving the family.

Jodadoh'gowah told his story of fulfilling the vision and relaxed, leaning back and snuggling into his wife's lap. He exhaled and allowed his eyes to wander to the upper supports of the long house.

Cannibal Woman was hovering in the rafters above his kin! Her yellow eyes glared through the smoke and her breathing made a rapid clicking sound like the noise a rattlesnake made before it struck. The creature said in a voice that only he could hear, "I'll visit you again next year." And she floated out the smoke hole.

****

The next morning, others were strong enough to dress for the hunt and follow his trail. Jodadoh'gowah stood outside the longhouse with his wife and held his daughter close against his chest, watching the hunters slowly wade through the snow to the bear den.

Neoge'deseno'sgwa blew tiny air kisses onto their daughter's forehead to make her smile and they knew that the Creator had borne her to his family a second time. Embracing her husband, she said, "The Maker of Life has blessed us, my love. He has given your spirit the gift of sight."

Jodadoh'gowah hugged his wife and daughter warmly, but his eyes drifted, staring beyond the hunters trudging through the snow, far off into the wilderness.

"Are you troubled?" she asked.

"It is a heavy burden to see dreams from the Creator," he said.

Neoge'deseno'sgwa thought for a moment and her face firmed. "The Maker speaks to us in mysterious ways," she said, "through the thundering break of a grouse, or the howl of a red wolf, sometimes the fireflies' night dances. We must not be afraid. He saved us by giving your dream the gift of sight. We must have faith."

Neoge'deseno'sgwa put a hand around the back of her husband's head and drew it against her neck. A wave of contentment engulfed Jodadoh'gowah and he wished the warm embrace would never end.

35.
Ropes, Ropes, and Ropes
The Gravel Mountain Ski Patrol Newsletter
Earl W. Wolfe

Lift Evacuation Ropes: Ski Area Management is very concerned about the uncontrolled use of these ropes by patrollers at Gravel Mountain.   Please, patrollers, these ropes are to be used for lift evacuations only.

The ski instructors complain that patrollers have been apologizing too many times for "accidentally clothes-lining" them. This occurs when patrollers ski down the slope, in parallel, ten to twenty feet apart, with the lift evacuation rope strung between them.   The patrollers claim that they do this for the teenagers who love to jump the rope as it approaches, and the technique requires a lot of practice to keep the rope close to the ground.

The instructors, unfortunately, unlike the teens, are normally facing downhill and unaware of the approaching rope. They claim that they receive the warning "look out" too late to duck.   Their normal reaction to the "look out" is to look uphill just in time to catch the rope at neck level.   This clothes-lining normally results in minimal damage, but the instructors occasionally suffer from a slight hoarseness (their turtle neck sweaters keep rope burns to a minimum.) Teenagers are coming to our area in increasing numbers to enjoy the sport of rope jumping and lift ticket sales are way up.   Our area manager also appreciates the associated income from their parent's attendance at the bar, but asks the patrollers to please avoid the ski instructors or give them a little more warning.

Sadly, on the other hand, inexperience and lack of accuracy in this sport resulted in two instructors catching ropes in their mouths last Saturday.   One lost his false teeth and had to cancel his class while spending two hours looking for them (relatively white teeth) in the (relatively) white snow. The other, in reflex action, clamped his teeth onto the rope and was carried backwards all the way down the hill. He actually bit ¼ of the way through the rope. The rope had to be replaced out of our party fund because the bite was in the middle of the rope and management blames us for the damage. Thanks to Patroller Carpenter who offered to have a small section of the subject rope (with the bite marks) bronzed and tastefully mounted on a mahogany plaque for the Patrol Lounge. Fortunately, Thumbs (our smallest patroller) has offered to repair the rope with a splice and we will use it only in training our new patrol candidates.

Toboggan Tail Ropes: The rescue toboggan tail ropes are causing problems. There seems to be a tendency for the dangling ends of the toboggan tail ropes to tie themselves into loops. Occasionally, when transporting a toboggan up to the top of the hill on the chair lift, (ski-mobiles busy elsewhere) the tail rope will come loose and dangle down from the seat of the chair. It is amazing how this seems to happen only when a ski instructor is standing directly under the lift cable.

It is equally amazing how the loop in the tail rope will drop over and catch on anything that the ski instructor has raised: hand, ski pole, hat, head, etc. This must stop!! Although several ski instructors have added inches to their height, their clothes had to be retailored to adjust for the physical "improvement". Your ski patrol has been billed to cover the tailoring bills: $373.14. This had to come out of the party fund.

Again, this must stop!! Our end-of-the season party fund is now down to $5,686.67. We are going to have to spend more time on the bunny hills and under the lifts looking for spilled change, cash, credit cards and jewelry. The following are not suggestions: Please, do not unintentionally run into patrons with money in their hands to accomplish associated spillage; no out-of control "accidental" collisions in front of the lodge with new skiers, and do not gently nudge beginners so that they will ski out of control and accomplish the desired goal.

Warning: Our Area owner and our Manager are threatening your ski patrol with lift evacuation and toboggan rope sensitivity training. Worse, they threaten to cut off access to our beer supply during that training. You know that our current refreshers were extended to cover other concerns that emerged over the years and we certainly don't want some supercilious community college graduate student lecturing to us for two or three dry and boring hours on how to be nicer to all non-patrollers. So, please ease off!!

36.
School's Out
Deborah Guzzi

Trying to recapture the joy of those winter days is difficult. School cancelled: the sun shining through the sheer white curtains into an all too girlie room, the sound of the teakettle's whistle, the ice cold feeling of oak boards on bare feet between scatter rugs as I ran to the kitchen. The transistor radio still babbled school closings as the snow sifted down.

bright sun
sparkles on snowflakes –
the plow roars

Quick phone calls, punctuated with giggles, rouse the gaggle of neighborhood girls. White skates in hand, I am out the door. I rush toward the swampy area behind the neighbor's house. My rubber boots crunching through the crust above the powdery fluff. At the edge of the watery wood I stand staring. Boys, I see the boys in there. They have their skates on already. Tommy Maloney, my crush, skates toward me.

his black waves
dusted with snow –
whoops of delight

A hummock of snow-topped grass serves as a seat. I remove my boots from beneath the zip sides of my snow pants and try to tie laces on my new white skates. Once done I stand wobbling, weak-ankled. Tommy laughs, as knock-kneed I attempt a glide toward him falling on my butt. Oh how his eyes sparkled, an Irish rogue at twelve. Kneeling, Tommy began to re-lace my skates. I remember wishing, so much, he would kiss me.

37.
Sensing Winter
A. J. Huffman

Shadows elongate, consume vision.
Surroundings dim, just a notch. Slight
gray seems to agree with chilled whispers
of the wind.

I. Seeing Winter

Pristine white of first snowfall's mantle. Branches and gutters
glistening, accessorized in ice. In absence
of disruptive activity, everything holds
its breath for a moment to enjoy the view.

II. Touching Winter

Gentle kiss of snowflake to lash. Shock
of wind slipping under skirt. Sting
of child's snowball connecting with neck,
back. Aching numbness
of fingers pulled from dampened gloves,
flared before warming flames of fireplace.

III. Hearing Winter

Trees turn mute, absent
of rustle and chirp. Abandoned,
stripped to slumbering bark.
Their shadows shiver with every crunch
of treaded bootfall, heavy
with possibility of ax. The silent pause
before echoing chop.

IV. Smelling Winter

Forested essence of pinecones gathered,
lingers when left
to dry by the fire. Sickly smoke
of sapling, accidentally tossed
into flame. Welcoming
wafts of fresh-baked bread resonating
from oven, the perfect welcome
home.

V. Tasting Winter

Tongue-burning first sip of cocoa, melting
mini-marshmallows, as the restless wait
for tell-tale ting that heralds plates
full of cookies. Chips oozing,
semi-molten chocolate coats tongue.
Cooled later with lick of peppermint
dress for the occasion, in holiday stripes.

38.
Sister, February 23, 2012
Ruth Sabath Rosenthal

End-Cut Prime Rib of Beef, Crab Cake,
Lobster Tail, Sea Scallops.
I feel — no — need to, eat the foods
you asked me to get for you.

So, I scour the internet for
Manhattan restaurant menus,
listing, first and foremost,
roast prime rib of beef,

confident that, if I find that,
the rest of your list gets checked off.
It's the Post House, on East 63rd Street,
that has everything.

And, on this day, the 1st anniversary
of your death, I eat the foods
you craved, yet I do not savor
a morsel. But not to worry, Renee,

for next year, same date, I'll try
again, and maybe, just maybe,
I'll find it easier to enjoy what
you surely would have, if only

I'd realized there was no time left.
No time left, as I held your hand
and watched American Idol
while you morphed into whatever it is one becomes at death.

39.
Sleeping In Saint Paul, MN
Taylor Burkard

I

My breath is cigarette smoke, watching the paper boy thump his boots
one in front of the other; cracking acorns with his foot teeth.
The street hissing fog, motionless and torpid before the car crash;

some bastard with Illinois plates, no one could see him at first through
his black windows.   They vacuumed the meat sauce with a truck taller than
Jesus of Nazareth. The street warms, its cracks pulsate with blood.

The mess is cleaned before I could put my pants on or say a Hail Mary.
This used to be a nice place, God lived just down the street,
said a man that wore a boyscout shirt from nineteen-seventy-one;

steak lodged in his teeth and he continues to spray toxic words,
Price of gas was cheap, before women and blacks could vote. I couldn't speak,
my mouth drowning in spit. He was abducted by the bus, I went back to sleep.

II

I hide in my building; the blank radio noises
ride the breeze and warn of another man dead.

People at work across state lines, pin memos to cork
that have nothing to do with humanity.   I can see

the Virgin Mary speaking soft American Sign Language
in my bathroom mirror, blisters forming on my fingers

from trying to sign back.   Only ghosts and alcoholics on Selby Avenue
come back tomorrow, I say.   The radiator clicks and the pipes

try to emulate the sound of dying trees.   I find a radio station that hums old news,
it's every eulogy ever written, I can't stay awake my eyes cemented by tears.

40.
Smoke In The Wind
J. P. Christiansen

There is this winter's wind.

A lone crow is on the wing, driftingly.

A great horned owl surveys the landscape from a bare branch, waiting for a critter bounty daring to cross the open frozen field asleep under a thin layer of hard snow.

A chimney's smoke guides me to the one who knows most about me.

41.
Snow Snakes
The Gravel Mountain Ski Patrol Newsletter
Earl W. Wolfe

We have an epidemic here at Gravel Mountain that was generated by some not-so-friendly practical-jokers, and your patrol board of directors and area management rightly call it sabotage! All of us are aware that the other local ski areas compete aggressively and unfairly with our beloved area for customers. There is a group of ski instructors and patrollers from those other areas that vacation and climb mountains in far-off portions of our globe. Their recent trip to climb and explore the Kirghaz Mountains of northern Siberia netted some interesting fauna known to inhabit the lower slopes of that range. Worse, they brought several pairs of the rare and squirmy devils back and let them loose at our area a year ago - last spring.

What am I talking about? I am talking about honest–to-goodness snow snakes! These are not mythical creatures dreamed up by alcohol fevered brains along with pink elephants and dancing crocodiles. They are real, and I have seen them and caught a few (snakes) myself.

A review of the biology of this invasive species is quite alarming: Like the Burmese pythons in Florida, they comfortably adapted to our climate and find plenty to eat. Rats, mice, frogs and toads are their regular diet; although rabbits, possums, small dogs and kittens will do if available. None have grown to a size that mothers need be concerned for the safety of their babies and small children - yet. The snow snakes are surviving and breeding in the swampy acreage at the back of our area. That area is now identified and protected by the National Forest Service because the NSA, EPA and NHTSA have listed them as an endangered species and quarantine the area to humans. They are considered to be at the same level of danger of extinction as snow leopards and white tigers.

Because of their heritage, they need not hibernate, but thrive in below freezing weather and frolic with the snowshoe rabbits on our snow-covered ski slopes after dark. They sprout white fur when the colors of autumn become heavy with frost, snowshoe rabbits turn to white and stoats become ermines. Since they are nocturnal and covered with white fur, they are invisible to the average viewer. The informed know where to look and the numbers they have counted on the slopes are rather appalling. The way they romp and cavort on the darkened slopes (i.e. gyre and gimble on the great white wabe (my pun)) is really quite amusing and diverting.

The major problem is that they burrow under the snow. Some burrows look like the tunnels generated by moles (more on the snow-moles later), but many tunnels are just deep enough under the surface of the snow that there is no visible hump. This latter often occurs when they dig in the snow during a snowstorm or when fresh snow is being laid down by the snow making machines. The tops of these tunnels easily collapse under the weight of the skier, and beginning and intermediate skiers and ski instructors can easily catch their skis in these curvy grooves. Worse, some of the snow snakes may overnight and sleep in their tunnels instead of sliding back home to their icy swamp. Can you imagine the yellow snow that develops when a slow skier breaks through and collapses a tunnel over a sleeping squirmer and the snake jumps up in alarm and wraps himself around the skier's legs?

The immediate correction to this concern is for all of our ski instructors and patrollers to form lines at the top of the hills and side-step down all of the hills before the area opens in the morning. Secondly, all disturbed snow snakes must be gently corralled, tagged and returned to the swamp. This exercise will be followed by slope groomers "polishing" the slopes for the customers.

The concern for the patrol is that there will be no "sleeping-in" anymore at our patrol chateau. Area management wants everyone at the top of the hills at seven in the morning, sharp! Learning of this management-imposed disaster, our French chefs, Henri and Fifi LaRousse, had hissy-fits and wept bitterly when they learned they would have to revise their breakfast routine-especially for weekends. Les crepes, les exquisite petit fours and les sausages aux Bourdeaux will not be aux estandard Francais until Fifi, and especially Henri, have adjusted to the revised starting time. Their excursions to the local markets have to be rescheduled too and they will no longer guarantee the absolute freshness of the vegetables, the eggs or the vintage of the Bourdeaux for les sausages. (Sigh).

This result of that saboteur-imposed outrageous atrocity must not go unpunished!!!

Your Board of Directors and area management have considered and discussed methods of retaliation rather extensively. Those who were literate made several trips to Encyclopedia Americana and Encyclopedia Britannica for clarification, of various chemistry, ecology, bio-diversity and potential for adversarial climate change retaliations. They have, together with several professors from our State universities and local colleges, come up with a list of several potential weapons for retaliation and retribution. None of the weapons have ingredients that can be traced back to any retaliatory practical jokers (saboteurs.) Fortunately, explosives (i.e: TNT & dynamite) although initially considered, were temporarily put on the back burner for last resort reconsideration. More later.

42.
Snow
Mark Hudson

The show goes on,
with or without snow.
Snow will always blow,
wherever I can go.
I could go somewhere
where the weather is warm.
But snow will be elsewhere,
in some shape or form.
The snowman sits in someone's yard
and has a carrot nose.
No one knows he has it hard,
he'll never smell a rose.
The snowman was a creature
the children used to make.
But now we see his features,
only by mistake.
The truth is many homes
sit in bad foreclosures,
like oh so many poems,
they've lost all exposure.
O snowman, Mr. Snowman,
come back to winter's eve.
You really do not know man,
that once I did believe.

43.
Street Lamp
Joann Grisetti

She held no fear of shadows
dark dancing on her wall and ceiling
where light from the street lamp shone.

She heard the music they danced by
and tapped her toes upon the sheets
in rhythm with the wind and leaves.

She sighed - no loss as they disappeared
in freezing nights, their going
gave longer time to sleep and dream.

She smelled the cold of winter
settle into bare branches through
the glass. She felt wiser than age five.

44.
Sugar Cookie Mornings
Deborah Guzzi

The silent snow sugared the street and across the concrete walk,
dry and weightless it swirled off hand across the concrete walk.

Virgin snow sprinkled clusters of burnt, butter-brown oak leaves
crisp
beneath the frost purpled hedgerows branded across the concrete
walk.

Perceptus precipitation frosts the rusted harrow in the field,
red it bleeds heart memories, once grand, across the concrete walk.

Frozen wind chimes tinkle in time remind of the sleigh bells ring;
call out to children with dreams in hand across the concrete walk.

Days before Christmas the baker performs on a sugar cookie morn,
dusting trees, the homes, the lawns unplanned across the concrete
walk.

45.
The Busted Watch
Edward Ahern

We'd spent our years together in guy-talk banalities, beneath which I think both Pete and I knew that it would end badly. The awareness of the ending started with a phone call.

"No George," I said."I haven't talked to Pete in at least three weeks, so I don't know what he's up to."

"Look Mike, I've tried calling and e-mailing him for over a week with no response. His voice mail is full. Something's wrong. I'm trapped into appointments until next week and can't get up there. He's your friend. Could you go up and check on him?"

"I squirmed for a few seconds. "Well, hell. All right, George, walk over and drop off the keys. I'll try to get hold of Pete and if I can't reach him I'll make the run up tomorrow."

I hung up and called Pete's number. The message box regurgitated on me. I fired off an e-mail that disappeared into the ether. George dropped off the key to what had been his childhood home.

The next morning I waited until the morning traffic congestion dwindled down. I had four hours to weave my way around trucks from southern Connecticut to Fall River, Massachusetts. Lots of time to think.Pete Harding and I had been get-drunk-together buddies, which meant we didn't have to believe each other, just back stop fantasies. We were unattached Caucasians living in Japan. Our limited Japanese made it hard to say anything significant to our neighbors, and we'd defaulted into closeness.

After three years we both bailed out and took corporate jobs stateside. Once I'd dried out and Pete hadn't we saw each other less frequently. Pete's fabrications had grated a lot more without the lubrication of booze. Over the next ten years Pete spiraled down through increasingly menial jobs and spent what little money he had.

"They're throw away jobs, Mike," he'd said. "But once I get something decent the first thing I'm going to do is take my Rolex out of the safe deposit box and get it fixed."

He'd sold or pawned everything else of value. The watch was the only thing left he could brag about. And even that was suspect. I'd never actually seen it. When Pete had been threatened with eviction from his two room apartment I'd arranged for Pete to take care of George's vacant family home in Fall River. I hadn't been there since I'd helped Pete move in.

Pete's car was in the driveway. I rang and knocked at the front door but there was no answer. The mailbox overflowed with letters and circulars. I unlocked the front door, but it was bolted from the inside. I walked through the snow covered yard to the back door. The key worked.

The smell ballooned out and pushed me back, a wave of throat rasping decay. I held my breath and stuck my head into the kitchen. It was full of flies, alive and dead. Even without breathing, the sweet/sour cloy oozed into my nostrils.

I slammed the door shut and dialed 911. A long five minutes later the squad car pulled up, followed by an ambulance and a fire truck. I wondered what the firemen would do. I explained to the cops who I was and what I'd done. One of the cops took the keys and reopened the back door. He backed away a lot faster than I had, but had the experience to leave the door open so the concentrated rot could dissipate. He turned to the other cop.

"Jesus, I hate these." Then he called over the EMTs." You'll need respirators and suits."

Four of them suited up and went in. A gust of wind reminded me how cold the day was, maybe five degrees below freezing. I went back to my car, put on my winter coat, and called George. "George, hi. Listen, I think Pete might have died in the house."

"Are you sure it's not just the refrigerator that's crapped out?"

"No, Pete's car is here, and the smell is awful, something's dead in there. I called the cops. They're in the house now. That's all I know, but I'll call you back once they come back out."

The EMTs came out first and starting getting out of their hazmat suits. I gave one of them a questioning look.

"Mr. Marteau, there's a body on the sofa in the TV room. Been dead a long time. There's maggots and flies all over and decomposition fluids have seeped through the sofa and into the carpet."

The two cops came back out, pulled off their respirators but left the overalls on. The cop I'd talked to, Royce Burrows, called the medical examiner's office. We organized coffee from a nearby diner while we waited. When the guy from the ME's office showed up he and the two cops dressed up and walked into the house.

The Medical examiner and first cop came out empty handed. The second cop came out carrying a body bag in one hand without leaning over from the weight. Once they'd stripped out of their suits I went over to Burrows.

"Is it Pete?"

"Dunno. The body's badly decomposed. The remains go to the ME's office for identification and a cause of death, although determining that will be tough. The heat in the house had been set high, around seventy five, which accelerated things. I turned the thermostat down to sixty.

"We have all your contact information, Mr. Marteau. Is there a next of kin?"

"Sort of. He has a bitter ex-wife in Oregon, and a sister he hasn't talked to in eight or nine years."

"We'll need their information. Once we've authorized entry the owner can go in and clean up. Whoever goes in there should get respirators and hazmat suits."

The second cop relocked the door and put warning tape on it. The vehicles cleared out of the yard and I was left alone in the snow. I called George.

"George, listen, they found a body in the TV room. Yeah, pretty sure it's Pete. The cops and Medical Examiner have been and gone. The place is locked up again and we can't get in until they give their okay. Do you have insurance for this? The cop said that the place would have to be stripped and decontaminated."

"Mike, is the house all right?"

"No, listen, shit, I don't know. The heat's still on, so there shouldn't be a problem with the pipes. Nothing else I can do here, so I'm coming back."

Fewer trucks clogged the road on the way back, but I missed them, they would have kept me busy maneuvering. Random thoughts fired off. How much Pete aggravated me. How I hated his constant lying about important people he knew and the important things he'd done. How I could be doing more for him. It was only when I wondered about the cause of his death that I realized I'd been thinking of Pete in the present tense.

I remembered the last fishing camp we stayed at. It was as close as I ever came to bracing Pete about his lies and as Pete ever got to being honest with me. The dead dark of Canadian forest swallowed the dim cabin lighting just outside the windows. We were both drunk.

"And after I came back from Japan I picked up an MBA while I was working out of Hartford."

"Bullshit Pete. I think you got an MBA just like I think you really met Henry Kissinger. Tell me the truth, for Christ's sake."

Pete stared at me, eyes bleared. "What do you know? You don't know what it's like to be completely broke, to have nothing, to be able to do nothing. You've got a wife, a job, money."

We'd stood on the threshold of his purgatory, me looking in and him looking out, but went back into hiding, talking about the next day's fishing.

I had to stop in at George's place before I went home. He'd grown up in the Fall River house that now was uninhabitable. He deserved a face to face apology from me for recommending Pete as a lodger.

"What the hell happened, Mike? Pete sounded drunk a couple times when I called. Was he an alcoholic?"

"Could be. He hadn't had anything good happen to him in a long time. His wife divorced him within a month of his losing his best job. He had gout and terrible eyesight, and was at least seventy pounds overweight. He'd lost his last job as a jitney driver about a month ago."

"He was broke? He always paid me."

"Flat. The only times Pete went out to eat was when I took him. He talked about a safe deposit box that had an expensive watch in it but I never saw it. Probably just another of his lies. Look George, I want to help you with this. Pete was my friend and not yours. I recommended him to you. We'll take care of things once the cops let us in."

The next day I dug up Pete's wife's telephone number and the name and location of Pete's sister. I called officer Burrows and the ME's office in Boston and passed along the information.

The ME's office called back a few days later. "Mr. Marteau, this is Jennifer Carson of the Medical Examiner's office in Boston."

"Yes?"

"I've contacted Mr. Harding's former wife and sister. Unfortunately neither one wishes to become involved with the disposition of Mr. Harding's remains. His sister was, um, quite firm that she would decline to have anything to do with his affairs. This means we have no next of kin to work through."

"I'm not surprised. They hadn't spoken in years."

"Mr. Marteau, we need someone to assume responsibility for Mr. Harding's burial once identification is confirmed."

"But I'm not his executor…"

"I understand Mr. Marteau, and it would be impossible for you to act as administrator of his affairs, since you reside out of state."

"Pete had no money. Doesn't the state just bury him?"

"The state may provide burial assistance, but we need a person to take responsibility for his burial. You don't have to be related to Mr. Harding to do this."

"Oh. Ah, there's no one else I know of, so I guess I'm it."

"Thank you Mr. Marteau, I'll e-mail you the forms. Based on our initial examination I believe the police will let you have entry to the house shortly. One thing though..."

"Yes?"

"We haven't been able to identify the body yet, because of its deteriorated condition. His dentures were missing. It would expedite matters if you could locate the dentures and forward them to us."

"How does that help identify him?"

"We match the contours of the dentures to the bone structure of his jaw."

"Dentures. Jesus. All right I guess."

I called Burrows and got his okay to go into the house. George and I drove to Home Depot. They had hazmat suits but no respirators, so we had to settle for masks with filters. The next day we drove up from Connecticut to Fall River.

I anticipated the stench, which made it worse. The mask and filters kept the flies from our faces, but did little to keep out the odor. Thousands of dead flies littered the floor and furniture. The latest generation of living flies was listless. There was nothing left for them to feed on. Soiled clothes and food remnants were strewed about the rooms. The garbage disposal in the kitchen was clogged with clam shells. We opened up doors and windows to the winter air.

The smell was worst in the TV room where Pete had died. An empty scotch bottle lay next to the couch, which was soaked in body fluids and retained the shape of his body. Pete had died while lying on his side. I held my breath three times to enter and reenter the room and shove open the windows. On my way out on the third trip I noticed Pete's car keys and wallet neatly placed on a yellow legal pad with some numbers written on it. I scooped them up as I left.

George started gathering family items while I bagged up Pete's personal effects from the bedroom and a desk in the living room. Pete had organized nothing. Bills, diplomas, photos were all jumbled into drawers. I grabbed handfuls of material from the drawers and threw them into a trash bag. I noticed two little envelopes for deposit box keys in the bottom of one drawer. There really was a safe deposit box. I loaded another trash bag with four weeks of mail from the front porch. I found the dentures tossed loose into a drawer in the bathroom and added them to the trash bag.

George was ominously silent, but compulsively reacted to the violation of his family kitchen. He spent two hours cleaning rotten food from the refrigerator and sink, and fly infested boxes from the cabinets. When we walked out just before dark the kitchen was the only room in the house that looked remotely habitable.

George blew up on the drive back to Connecticut. "How could he treat my house like that! Not his dying, the way he was living. Rooms filthy, food left to rot on the stove. The bathtub was filled with dirty underwear!"

"I know. And I recommended him. But God help me, he was my friend, George. He was a broke drunk with no job, and bad health problems. The last time I saw him he could barely walk. His sister and ex-wife hated him. Maybe he just gave up."

But George deserved to be let in a little more. "As his life got worse he compensated by fabricating stories about what he'd accomplished and who he knew. It got so I didn't believe anything he told me. I liked him in spite of it all, by osmosis maybe, or because of who he once was. And God help me I still like him, for all that he did to you and the money he borrowed from me that I'll never see again."

After I dropped George off I was too tense to vegetate. I spent the evening going through Pete's effects. He'd jettisoned most of the records of his life. There was only one picture of his parents, two of his ex-wife., and none of his sister. There was no will or instructions on what he wanted done after his death. He had a few dollars in a savings account, and one dollar bill in his wallet. He owed about $30,000 to credit unions, banks, doctors and hospitals. He was the most improved student in the third grade of St. Margaret's school. He graduated with an MBA from a well-known business school. One for you, Pete, you did tell the truth sometimes.

There was a severance letter from his last company advising that he was being fired from his minimum wage job because, for the third time, he had hit a parked car with his service truck. I realized that Pete must have concealed the loss of sight in his right eye.

A yellow legal pad had handwritten numbers listing his income and expenses for the coming month. Without his check from the livery company he was below water by $350. I called a recommended undertaker in Fall River the next day. He was nicer than he had to be, given that Pete would be buried with $1200 in State assistance in an unmarked pauper's grave. The death certificate arrived a week later in the mail. The cause of death was listed as heart failure, which I assumed was their wild assed guess. After I'd talked again to the undertaker I called Camille, Pete's sister. "Camille, I appreciate your talking with me. I know you and Pete weren't close."

"He was dead to me a long time before he died. I don't want anything to do with him, alive or dead. Just send me a copy of the death certificate."

"Pete could be hard to put up with."

Camille's voice broke. "He was a thief and an ingrate. I took care of our dad and mom when they got sick and died and he never helped out, never sent money or came to visit. And then after they were dead he went to the house and took stuff. How can you be his friend?"

"I sometimes ask myself that, Camille. When we were drinking buddies we were okay with each other. Later on he was, I don't know, part of me that wasn't surviving, that needed protection."

Pete's ex-wife Rose was also scarred over. "Mike, I never told you, but Pete lost his job in Hartford because of his drinking. And he got worse. Pete was nice around you, but he was abusive when he drank. Even after we got divorced he would get drunk, call me and make threats. I can send you a little money to help with the burial but leave me out of it."

"Do you want me to send his papers? There isn't much."

"No, don't. There's nothing I want. Mike, for what it's worth, Pete seemed to be happiest when you and he were fishing together. It was like he could take some time out from a bad life."

I scraped together some money from Pete's acquaintances and another $300 of my own and got him buried. I mailed copies of the death certificate to the creditors, telling them that Pete had died broke and not to contact me. Three of them tried to reach me anyway. I told the car loan company where to collect the car and keys. And that left just the safe deposit box.

Carol Groves was in charge of the safe deposit boxes at the bank. "Mr. Marteau, Mr. Harding was the only signatory with access to the box. Although you have the keys you're not the administrator of his estate, so you have no access. If, as you say he has a sister she can petition for access to the box."

"She wants nothing to do with his affairs. What happens once the rent isn't paid on the box?"

"We open it and turn the contents over to the State."

"I'll call you back."

I called Rose first. "Listen, Pete apparently has a safe deposit box. The only thing that's maybe in it is a busted watch. I can't get into it, and from out in Oregon I don't know that you can or want to get involved, but I wanted to tell you about it."

"Safe Deposit Box?"

"Yeah. I've got the keys but only Pete could have used them. His sister could spend some money and get the right to open the box, but I don't think she wants to go anywhere near it."

"Pete had money our first few years together, but after all he's been through I can't believe there's anything left. Do what you need to do, Mike."

Camille didn't hesitate. "Nothing, I want nothing to do with him Mike. Least of all going through the legal expense and aggravation of trying to get into a bank box."

"I don't know what's in there Camille, maybe his will, maybe an old Rolex, maybe nothing. If you're sure I'll just turn the keys back in to the bank."

"Do it." Camille hesitated. "You've were a good friend to him Mike. Too good. He always thought he was better than me, smarter, better educated. Look at him now."

"Yeah."

I called Carol Groves back at the bank. "Carol, I'm going to send you a letter with the keys and a copy of the death certificate. A favor to ask though."

"As I said, Mr. Marteau, you have no access to the box."

"I understand, but we should know what was in the box, just to settle things. Could you give me a call back and let me know?"

"I guess so."

George and I spent three days stripping his family home of its furnishings, most of which were consigned to a dumpster. We bricked up the experience, and never mention how and where Pete died.

It took two more months for Carol Groves to call back. "Mr. Marteau?"

"Yes?"

"Carol Groves from the bank. We opened the box. The only thing in the box was a watch."

"No will?"

"No. The watch apparently is an eighteen caret solid gold Rolex. It'll get turned over to the State."

I smiled. Busted Pete and his busted Rolex were both being taken care of by the State. Better care than maybe I'd been able to give him. I waited a year, but no one contacted me, so I burned his photos and papers. I couldn't bring myself to just throw them out. I keep his wallet in the center drawer of my desk, where I see it fairly often. I left the lone dollar bill inside it. A leather keepsake from a good friend with no gravestone.

46.
The First Falling
A.J. Huffman

Powder.
The softest snow.
Perfectly packable.
Ammunition balls and snowmen
are born.

47.
The Indian In The Hills
Nasy Sankagiri

Sunny Iyengar woke up early that morning, like any other day. He sat up in bed, with both feet firmly on the ground. The bed was oriented so that he sat up facing East. He folded his hands in salutation and bowed his head in silent prayer – to the Sun, to the world, to the creation. This too was a daily ritual like waking early, performed without much thought, ingrained into him over the past twenty five years.

After completing his ablutions, Sunny walked into the kitchen and made coffee with practiced efficiency. He spooned out equal amounts of three different coffee beans from three separate jars into the coffee grinder. The grinder was within a custom made silencing chamber – Sunny seriously disliked the noise of the coffee grinder. He poured the coarse powder into the conical filter of the coffee maker, added bottled spring water, and turned it on. He went and sat in his Lay-Z- Boy leather recliner, waiting for the coffee. The coffee maker gurgled like a little infant that was tickled by its dad. It was a happy sound – a good sound to greet the new born day. Sunny's eyes surveyed the apartment.

It was a small apartment, but decorated in a contemporary style, reflecting Sunny's taste as well as personality – orderly, rational and practical. Nothing fanciful. When the coffee was ready, Sunny filled his mug and returned to the recliner. All around him was quiet. It was as if the city that had been screaming itself hoarse throughout the night had finally fallen silent to catch its breath, just for a couple of hours. Enjoyment of coffee occupied Sunny fully and completely for the next few minutes. The morning coffee was a relatively new habit that Sunny had cultivated with his usual deliberate precision, unprompted by his father or the rigors of his professional life. It was the one time he surrendered to pure sensory bliss. Savoring the caffeine induced gentle buzz in his head,

Sunny focused on the day ahead. It was a big day for him. Vice President at twenty nine! He had called his father in Los Angeles the previous night with the good news. His father was proud of him. Sunny placed the empty mug in the sink and went over to the big window. He parted the blinds and looked eastward. It was late January, and the first rays of the Sun were trying to pierce through the dense fog. As he continued to stare, the fog seemed to melt away and he was able to see everything with utmost clarity. The clarity did not hit him, like some extraterrestrial punch – rather, it was like a gentle awakening. He looked at the red ball of the rising Sun and nodded, acknowledging its summons. He packed a small duffel bag, threw it into the passenger seat of the Honda CRV, got in and pulled out into the street. He did not stop at the BART station from which he usually took the train to his office. He drove past it and soon merged on to Lincoln Highway, drove past Oakland and headed into the open country, eastward.

****

Venkat Sundaram Iyengar migrated to the United States from India to work as a research scientist in the Bell Labs in New Jersey. He moved his young family to the US much against the wishes of his orthodox parents who considered crossing the ocean a sin. However, he still followed tradition in naming his son after his father. Venkat was determined that little Sundaram would have every advantage of growing up in the United States of America. He researched and planned everything. First, the name – Sundaram simply would not do. So, Indian Sundaram became American Sunny. Research showed that infants listening to classical music grew up to be high achievers. Boxed sets of various classical symphonies replaced the South Indian Carnatic music cassettes given by Venkat's mother.

He bought only the toys most suited for brain development. He was not like typical Indian parents who forced their children always to study and did not allow any play. Research showed that carefully chosen physical exercise as well as music complemented school learning and stimulated the brain. Therefore, Sunny was enrolled in a few select sports and Suzuki violin lessons, right from Kindergarten.

****

Sunny approached Reno around ten o'clock, but was not tempted to stop there. The artificial glitter of the casinos and the strip did not entice him. He stopped briefly at a rest stop further along the highway, just to relieve himself and stretch his legs a bit. The high desert stretched in all four directions as far as the eye could see. The traffic had thinned out. He got back on the road and reached the tiny town of Winnemucca at one o'clock in the afternoon. When he saw the city's sign on the outskirts, he remembered a line he had read on some travel website – Winnemucca, the oasis of the high desert! He decided to sample the oasis for lunch. Lunch was just a grilled vegetable sandwich and a bag of chips, which he ate sitting on a park bench. The January cold had a nip, but the Sun, high in the clear sky was warming up everything that he touched with his rays. It was nice, but he did not linger. *Eastward ho!*

****

When Sunny was about seven, Sunny's mother insisted on paying a visit to see her ageing parents in Chennai. She wanted to take Sunny also, but Venkat was extremely reluctant to let the boy go, because he had planned every minute of the summer for Sunny's development and growth. Moreover, he was concerned that Sunny's growth would be adversely affected by the chaotic and emotional nature of South Indian homes. However, he had to bow down to the pressure from the grandparents and reluctantly allowed Sunny to go for two weeks.

Sunny could not blend in with the brood of boisterous cousins, nor did he like much the invasion into his space by the bevy of aunts who insisted on hugs, kisses, pinching his cheeks and such sundry travesties. He would have gladly gone back to the US within that first week if someone gave him the chance. Then he discovered the music class his grandmother taught at home and fell in love with it. Venkat's mother was a respected teacher of South Indian music called Carnatic music. Sunny had a good ear, already well-tuned in his violin class. The grandmother noticed him hovering shyly around the class and gently coaxed him to join. He liked the little girls that came to class wearing colorful long skirts with shiny tinsel hems. He liked their immature voices trying to articulate the complex melodies, repeating after the teacher. He liked the melodic structure of the raga system; he liked the orderliness of each composition set in a distinct modal scale. He was instinctively drawn to the Raga Mohana, an enchanting pentatonic scale.

Sunny and his mother did not return to the US after two weeks. First one grandmother fell ill. They couldn't leave when the old lady was sick. When she got better, and they started packing, the other grandfather fell ill. Of course, they couldn't leave then because that would be disrespectful. Venkat was upset, but there wasn't much he could do under the circumstances. Sunny and his mother returned to New Jersey just in time for school. Sunny's mother tried to find a local teacher to continue his Carnatic music lessons, but Venkat would have none of it. There was no research to show any beneficial effects of Carnatic music on a boy's growth. The matter rested there.

****

It was quite dark by the time Sunny reached Salt Lake City. As the Honda cruised along Interstate 80, cutting through the heart of the city, he thought of the nice cafes of downtown, and was tempted to stop there for the night. However, the mysterious pull from the East wouldn't let him. He made a quick stop at a gas station to fill up and got back on the road. It started to snow. As he climbed higher into the mountains, the snow got heavier and the wind blew stronger. All the traffic moved at a cautious forty miles per hour. Some of the semi-trailers pulled over to the shoulder, and the drivers were putting snow chains on the tires.

Going into Summit Pass just before Park City, the snow got so heavy that visibility was almost zero. Huge blobs of semi-wet snow fell as if being hurled by a team of all-star baseball pitchers. The wipers struggled valiantly to keep the window clear, but the snow continued to cake up on the periphery. The Honda skidded once on a hair pin bend. Sunny was not used driving in such conditions, and he got scared for a minute. He was cold, tired and hungry. The larger SUVs, pick-ups and semis that were chained up whizzed past in the left lane. *Did I embark on this journey just to meet my end in these snowy mountains?* he wondered. However, stopping was not an option. He had to keep going. He knew that Park City was less than ten miles away.

It took him a little over forty minutes to cross the ten miles of the snow laden pass. Even as he contemplated taking the exit into Park City, the Honda emerged from the pass and the snow had suddenly let up. His spirits picked up too. He stayed on the highway.

****

Had Venkat been an educational researcher, he could have published several papers in scholarly journals on the benefits of the American scholastic system. After all, Sunny was the living example of it. He graduated high school at the top of his class and was the valedictorian. He maintained just sufficient interest in music and sports to keep his mind and body sharp. He graduated with honors from Princeton in Computer Science and got his MBA from University of Chicago. From there, Sunny's career progressed along a predictable trajectory. He made rapid advances in his job with his disciplined rational approach and methodical precision. Venkat was very proud of his American son – Sunny wouldn't do anything that is not rational. Vice President at twenty nine!

****

He could not remember the last time he had seen another vehicle on the road. The landscape was afloat in the ethereal glow of the pale moonlight. The earth was completely flat. He glanced at the clock. 10.37 PM. It occurred to him that perhaps he should stop for the night somewhere. A green exit sign came up after ten minutes. "Green River" it said. There were comforting and inviting symbols of food and bed under the sign.

What is this place? Looks like middle of nowhere. I wonder if it would be safe to stop here for the night, Sunny wondered. Immediately he chuckled to himself – *Safe? I've never done anything like what I did today. After what happened in that mountain pass, what am I afraid of?* Gosh, I am tired!

Even as he made the decision to stop for the night, the road curved sharply to the left and two enormous columns of eroded rock loomed ahead. The landscape changed dramatically from the featureless infinite flatness of high desert into rock formations, carved into fantastic profiles by centuries of erosion, and appeared spectacular in the dim light of the pale moon. He found it difficult to keep his eyes on the road. Within a minute, the car crested the peak of the mesa and emerged on top. To the right, he saw a wide valley which nestled the town with hundreds of lights glittering in the darkness like fireflies. It was at once surreal and beautiful. Then came the exit.

The exit ramp led into what seemed like the center part of the town on a two lane road. There were some official looking buildings and some shop fronts. The street was deserted. He passed a solitary blinking traffic light and spotted a gas station that was brilliantly lit. He didn't need gas, but thought this would be a good spot to get some information on where to stay and perhaps get something to eat. As he entered the store, the young man who was watching something on TV behind the counter, got up and came forward. The young man gave him a strange look.

"You're not from around here." It was a statement, not a question. Sunny was a bit taken aback, but nodded his head in assent.

"True, I'm from San Francisco."

"No, that's not what I meant. You don't look American!"

This really shook Sunny up. *I don't believe this! Should I stand here and explain to this dimwit that I am as American as him? Oh god, I am so tired,* Sunny thought. "My parents are from India," he said out loud in a non-committal way.

"Ohh! So, you are an Indian from India, then! Not like an Indian Indian, you know what I mean? There are many of those here, you know!"

"Hmm, whatever. Could you tell me if there's a hotel or a motel nearby?"

"Yeah, sure. There are a couple of motels down the road. They are Indians from India too, just like you. So, you should feel right at home."

He bought a bag of trailmix and walked back to his car. Getting back on the main street, he noticed two motels, one on either side of the road. He pulled into the one on the right. A neon sign in the parking lot proclaimed that the place had vacancy. A painted notice pointed to a dimly lit window as "office". The middle aged Indian woman with a sour face behind the window gave him a curious look.

Oh great! Now she'd want to know what a nice Indian boy like me is doing in the middle of the night! Sunny groaned to himself. But the woman just swiped his credit card and handed him the room key. She did not express any interest to engage him in conversation, and he was thankful for that. He got his duffel bag out of the Honda, walked into the room, stretched out on the bed and promptly fell asleep.

****

He got up when a ray of sunlight stabbed him in the eye. He woke with a start and could not understand where he was. The window seemed to be facing East, and though the drapes were drawn, there was a narrow gap which allowed the offending ray of light into the room. It took him a minute to remember where he was. The bed was saggy and his back was in agony. He got up gingerly and stretched himself. He felt much better after a long hot shower. After surrendering the room key to the middle aged Indian man in the office, he got into the Honda and sat in the driver's seat, just staring ahead. It was surprisingly not very cold in the car. The car clock said it was 10:14.

I'd better get going, he thought, yet he continued to sit there. He opened the bag of trailmix he had bought the previous day, and started munching one piece at a time. He was facing East. There was a mesa in front of him and he could see Interstate 80 and the traffic on it. The Sun was fairly high in the sky. As he continued to munch, he ran his gaze along the length of the mesa. His attention was drawn to a large rock formation that looked like some gigantic modern art sculpture. The oddly cylindrical rock glowed in multiple reddish hues wherever the sunlight touched it. He kept staring at it. He was entranced by it. Suddenly, he started the car, put it into gear and started driving towards the rock formation.

It was a fairly steep climb, but the road though unpaved, was good and the Honda made it there fairly easily. There was a small parking lot. It looked like this rock was a bit of a tourist attraction. The base of the rock was about thirty feet above the parking lot. He got out of the Honda and started climbing over the rough ground. By the time he reached the base of the rock, he was quite winded. It was cold and slightly breezy. The sun was shining brilliantly in a cloudless blue sky. It was not a single rock – rather it was a piece of the mesa that had been cut away from the main chunk, and then shaped by centuries of erosion by wind, rain and snow. He could see the various layers on the surface and each layer was a different reddish hue. Once he caught his breath, he walked around the rock to the other side.

On one side, he could see Interstate 80 far below, winding its merry way westward, through the spectacular rock pillars that he drove past the previous night. Those pillars too were carved by nature just like the rock next to him. The scene on the far side knocked his breath away. It was unlike anything he had ever seen. It was as if the Earth's skin had a case of goosebumps and they just froze like that. There were a few rocks jutting out here and there and there were clumps of occasional sage brush. The air was mildly fragrant with the aroma of sage. He left the big rock and started walking towards the frozen waves.

He went on walking, fully captivated by the landscape. It got to be very windy. Sunny had no track of time nor was he aware of his tired body. At times, the wind seemed to speak to him, goading him on. Suddenly, the world became very dark. Sunny stopped and looked at the sky. A humongous black cloud swallowed up the Sun. He shivered involuntarily. He looked around as if waking from a dream. He could not see the large rock from which he had set out. *When did I set out from that rock? How far had I walked?* he asked himself in disbelief, but curiously enough, he was not afraid. It was as if his adventures yesterday removed any sense of fear in him. There seemed to be a reason why he had stopped in Green River for the night. He was meant to come to this place. The wind told him that.

Suddenly, the wind turned into twirling gusts and sand began to fly with it. It began to prick the exposed skin of his face. He got down into a crouched position and drew his face into the partial cover of his jacket. His head was still exposed and he continued to feel the prick of the sand with the random gusts of wind. He thought he heard the sound of hoof beats coming from afar, but he couldn't be sure. The wind had been making some weird noises. He couldn't quite risk taking his face out of the jacket to have a look.

The sound of hoof beats became distinct, and they were a lot closer now. Almost as if by magic, the gusts subsided and the flying sand began to settle down. He stood up and shook his head and shoulders vigorously to shake off the sand. It was still quite dark and the black cloud still blocked out the sun. The air was thick with settling dust. In that unnatural twilight, he spotted a vague shape bouncing along at a distance, but could not be quite sure. Just then, the wind turned again and he could distinctly hear the sound of hoof beats, much nearer now. In a few seconds, the dust curtains parted in front of him and he saw a strange looking man riding towards him on a large horse. Sunny observed that, by facial features, the rider was some sort of a Native American. The rider wore dirty denim jeans and a denim shirt and rode without a saddle. He had long hair, but except for that, the rider did not display any other signs of his tribe.

The horse came to a stop a few feet away from Sunny. He stared at the rider, and the rider returned the gaze. The rider said something in an unfamiliar tongue. Sunny first thought he was asking something, but the rider's face did not seem inquisitive. Sunny merely shook his head to indicate he could not understand. The rider gave a nod, got down from the horse and started walking, holding the reins. Sunny followed him. Shortly they arrived at a big rock which was almost like a hill. It had a shallow cave, and the rider motioned to Sunny to sit inside the cave. The horse just stood there, without being tethered to anything. The rider pulled out a few dry sage clumps from the earth nearby and brought them into the cave. He knelt beside the pile of twigs and began to strike two flint stones. Sunny watched him with interest. Soon, the cotton caught fire and the rider laid it on the pile of twigs. The twigs caught fire, and a thin plume of sage smoke rose up in a curvy path, filling the cave with a gentle aroma. The rider sat down opposite him and drew some materials out of various pockets. Many questions popped up in Sunny – *What is this strange man doing alone in this magical place? Is he real? Well, the fire is real enough! What is he up to now?*

The rider filled a pipe with some tobacco and some other ingredients and lit it with a burning twig. He puffed on it till it caught and passed it on to Sunny. He shook his head declining the offer, but the rider was insistent. So, Sunny accepted the pipe and just held it. The rider mimed with action that he should take a strong pull. Sunny did so, and almost choked on the smoke. He was caught up in a fit of violent coughing. The rider clapped his hands in glee and was laughing merrily. Sunny saw all this through his coughing and teary eyes. The rider continued to laugh gleefully, like a child enjoying its prank. Sunny was very angry and wanted to throw the burning pipe in the rider's face, but was too consumed by the cough. As soon as he recovered from the coughing fit, the rider stopped laughing and mimed to him to take another pull on the pipe, and he did so. Then, Sunny felt his anger dissolve into the exhaled pipe smoke. The rider nodded in approval and said something in his strange tongue. He seemed to be congratulating Sunny, perhaps for getting the knack of the pipe or perhaps for his new beginning. Sunny took another pull on the pipe.

The rider leaned back against the rock and began to sing in a guttural voice. Sunny too leaned back against his side of the cave and closed his eyes. He felt his hearing grow very keen, picking up subtle nuances in the guttural singing – peculiar vibratos and surreal harmonies. The song blended into the plume of sage smoke and began to encircle him. It all began to feel natural and familiar to Sunny. The melody emerged fully formed and utterly beautiful. He knew this melody. It was Raga Mohana, which he had learned as a child from his music teacher grandmother in India. He surrendered his soul to it and it blessed his voice. He began to sing.

****

The next thing Sunny knew, he was climbing from the big colorful rock down to the parking lot. There was no sign of a cloud in the sky, and the Sun was a giant ball of orange red to the southwest. He could see the street lights come on in the small town in the valley below. He got into the Honda and drove onto Interstate 80, heading westward, heading home. He drove all night and reached home just before six. The first thing he did upon entering his apartment was to call his father. That's when he got the news that his grandmother had passed away in India. He went to the window, parted the drapes and stared at the Sun rising in the east. He felt touched.

48.
The Pelt
John Fitzpatrick

A hunter comes to check his traps.
He mistakes me for dead.
I am only asleep -- my way to handle pain.
I dream he carries me home
slung over his shoulder.

There, he throws me on a table.
First, on my belly,
then on my backside.
His cold steel knife starts
the long midriff cut. Its line

beads red. One bead appears, then another.
My insides spill through the opening,
molten lava that explodes over the rim,
colours bursting from closure of darkness,
crimson, darker tubular browns,

pale lines of tendrils steaming.
I am drawn from my covering,
a child taken from night's warm clothing,
my feet from their skin shoes,
my head aching from its delivery,

eyes from their concave lids.
He hangs me up to dry,
fastens me with nails.
But I am not there.
I begin to wake from my dream,

to feel a new life
only to find
I lie throbbing on the table
torn from myself
admiring my illustrious coat
hanging before me.

49.
The Sound of One Snowflake Falling
John Fitzpatrick

In silence, it falls.
Descends in rhythm
of flow.   Moves wherever

taken by wind or other force.
Does it express awe
at its landing after

distant journey? Giggle
when it bumps into another
like a child in random play?

Gibber with those who gather
as at a social feast? Perhaps
scream as another

and another and another pile
on top, shaping mounds
only agile can achieve?

Or sigh in joy
it has this moment
not knowing time

is short and another
will not come? It falls,
in silence, wanting

to feel at home in this new place,
to speak to someone,
some kind, another species.
I listen for sound. Yearn to reply.

50.
The South Dakota Blizzard
Mark Hudson

The South Dakota Blizzard was a giant battle,
the storm killed 80,000 cattle.
South Dakota rancher Scott Reder,
was just a typical farmer and breeder.
Breeding cattle was his bread and butter,
but now all he can do is mutter.
His ancestors owned this land forever,
now it seems like a hopeless endeavor.
The blizzard came early in fall,
and snowstorms blew through it all.
Maybe the dead cows are an obvious sign,
that winter is something that cannot be benign.

51.
The Troll Of Pine Knoll
J. P. Christiansen

We're sitting around the cabin fireplace.

My thoughts are on the troll
waiting on the knoll of pines –
he calls me to don my skis
and come pay him a visit.

Outside,
in Norwegian woods,
the temp is a perfect minus ten,
just right for a ski-run rendezvous.

It's about a half-mile climb
on the trail I know so well –
a gentle ascent through stillness
into knowing.

Moon lights up a white landscape.

The wax is still good on the skis –
staves are extensions of my arms,
the snow packed for easy progress.

When I reach the knoll of pines,
I sit down on a fallen log.
I light my pipe and wait.

I see smoke rising from our chimney
where humans seek each other.
I know about them.

A rustle focuses me.

"Hello!"

Night opens with a voice from
between cracks of rocks on the fjeld
resting in the complete silence of winter.

...

I return to the cabin about two am
to find the others waiting by the door.

"Where have you been?" they ask –
"we worried something happened to you."

It did.

52.
The Logophile's Longiloquence
Donna McLaughlin Schwender

Sunday mornings were holy to Maggie McDonald for sacrilegious reasons. A freshly fluffed featherbed was her pew, coconut coffee her Communion wine, and The New York Times crossword puzzle her hymnal.

Whether it was quirky or part of her religious practice, Maggie always had to start with the clue for thirteen, regardless if it was across or down. She also had to be drinking from the coffee mug that outwardly professed her "Word Nerd" status and whose innards bore the foxing of a treasured old book. Today was going to be no different.

Across
13. The Prioress's sweet dog food

As Maggie was descended from a long line of both maternal and paternal logophiles—many of whom had become English teachers or librarians—she offered a heavenly thank you to her grandmother for having introduced her to wastel, the six-letter answer. A lover of both the sight and sound of words, Granny McDonald had luxuriated in lulling her visiting grandchildren to sleep with the Middle English rhythm of Chaucer's Canterbury Tales. Maggie didn't always understand the ancient dialect—which was made even more difficult to decipher due to her grandmother's gammicism, but she identified with Madame Eglantine's love for animals.

She was so charitable and so pitous
She wolde wepe, if that she saugh a mous
Kaught in a trappe, if it were deed or bledde.
Of smale houndes hadde she that she fedde
With rosted flessh, or milk and wastel-breed.

Maggie was fortunate to also have had a mother who was a fabulist who further indulged her fondness for wildlife, as well as wild words, during their nightly story hour. The parables of her mother's creation had been woven into a solitary black leather book whose yapp binding reminded Maggie of the finest Bible. Having been exposed to large words while still in the womb, she was a young adult before she realized the stories were far removed from what most people would consider typical childhood ones.

Maggie felt blessed to have inherited the tome. Overwhelmed with the number of "LOL" and "OMG" type messages she was subjected to on a daily basis, she often needed a reminder of how lush language could be. It was then that she would treat herself to a tale or two.

Her favorite story began on page thirty-one. She had read it so many times, she could recite it verbatim in her mind. She simply held the book in her hands as if in prayer.

The Venator and the Xanthippe

There once was a retired daedalist who spent his earthbound days honing his skills as a bacchanal man. Unfortunately, his love of liquor laced his conversations with cacoephy. People who felt the need to correct his slurred speech only succeeded at increasing his lassitude for the human population.

Weary of their pompous echolalia, he decided to spend the remainder of his days roaming amongst the animals of the world—a whiskey bottle in one hand and a shotgun in the other. He would redeem himself before his family and friends as a salutary venator; the one who finally slew the town's legendary beast whose emergence from its cave was an undecennial event that began with the first snowfall of the season. Its reign of terror would continue until it managed to capture eleven of the townspeople's beloved pets—one for each year of its self-imposed exile from the world. No carcasses had ever been recovered during the creature's previous excursions, so no one knew for certain what had happened to the dogs, cats, rabbits, chickens, and one poor old donkey named Duffy that had been led astray.

Although considered a tacenda, during hushed discussions the demon was rumored to stand eight-feet tall and to be fleshed with a frightening fusion of feathers, fur, and scales. It was also feared that the hot-headed ignivomous monster was actually an oecist of an entire race of cave-dwelling behemoths.

As fall disappeared under the blanket of snow that began to coat the town's fear, the wannabe hunter and his intoxicating hamartia staggered off into the forest. It wasn't long before he came upon a trail of footprints. In his liquefied state of mind, the pelmatogram was not one he recognized.

As no amount of wind or snow could purge or absorb the alcohol from his sweating pores, he continued to lurch along as he followed the tracks. A deeply rooted kakorrhaphiophobia—one that had tethered him to the Earth during his days spent soaring in the air—drove him onwards to what he envisioned would be a magnality no one would ever forget. Success must win out over fear was his muttered mantra.

At the same moment that numbness consumed his ungloved trigger finger, the ogre appeared in his line of sight. At least such was the zooscopy that played out in his half-frozen, half-pickled mind. Unbeknownst to him, he had actually been following the footprints of his neighbor—the town's infamous xanthippe. A raffish quadragenarian who patrolled the perimeter of her property to rid it of rogue hunters, she threatened to abacinate any trespassers she detained; a blind fool would never dare cross her path again.

Possessing the ears of an owl, the vision of an eagle, and the speed of a cheetah, the suspected savage spun around to face her stalker - the jambiya strapped to her calf now held high over her head. At the same moment the double-edged blade sliced through the drunken interloper's soggy chest, the sluggish shotgun shell pierced the chimera's coat.

It only seemed fitting that the town's necrographer was the one to discover their lifeless bodies. While his written words tried to give meaning to their lives, it was his spoken words that gave birth to this tale.

The moral of the story: Those who go hunting for trouble will likely find it.

Genuflecting her head to the folio of fables, Maggie sighed at the thought that children's tales weren't written like that anymore. The realization that perhaps no one other than her mother ever really had was almost more than she could fathom. As the square paper boxes of her Sunday missal began petitioning her attention, she joyfully offered up a prayer for having been gifted with a life that read like a dictionary—full of meaning and unabridged.

53.
The Sleepers
Deborah Guzzi

The garden was bedded-down for winter.
Crisp white sheets drawn up and snugged,
about the heads of flaccid lettuce.

The tomato baskets stood erect
above the bridal bower of fertile soil.
Their legs bent humbly, they stood guard
like earthly warriors, at the entrance
to the King's chambers.

Remnants of spring and summer abundance,
battled the breezes, buoyed aloft,
on these metallic Tin men.

Beside the down deep, covered bed,
a path runs, buried beneath
the tossed off blanket of snow.
Upon the gray slate, already calf-deep
with snow, new snow falls,
soon to be marred by the harsh
tread of man, and the padded paws
of cat, skunk and possum.

Across the silvery surface,
these somnambulant creatures amble;
upon feet, both large and small.
The smaller beasts prater poignantly,
on breast-like mounds.
Pecking and pawing at the small
bare, brown, expanses
like lovers.

The covers are tossed aside,
scattered by shovel and salt,
and into the surreal bedroom
walks the groom, Winter,
yet again.

Doggedly, sprinkling the last his sleepers,
into the closed eyes of dreaming daisies.
Gamely, adorning vine and bough
in ice rivaling the finest Austrian crystal.
He leaves softly, silently, wishing his Bride
sweet dreams of Spring.

54.
Till Winter
Michelle Cacho-Negrete

It was barely dawn when Maggie's scratching at the door woke Leah who reached over to poke Doc and touched empty space instead. One month. She rolled over to press her face into his pillowcase, still unwashed; imagining some faint scent of him lingered, and ran her hand over the mattress as though some residual warmth had been retained. Leah had been certain that she'd die without Doc's soft, even breathing to set the pace of each day; she didn't. Life happened all around her, dragging her into it. The sun still rose, the dog still needed to go out, the shopping and laundry and bill paying still had to be done.

The faint sound ocean waves, usually masked by passing cars, indicated it was early, although she didn't know how early. Doc took a particular pride in his innate sense of time, outlawing a bedroom clock. He insisted he had "a handle on time." Not Leah. Since his death, time had shifted crazily out of control, night when it should be day, three in the morning instead of six, a month suddenly gone; she needed to become her own timekeeper and somehow put the hours right. She should buy a clock, but this simple act gave her pause; if she woke in the morning to its ticking, she'd lose those few precious, groggy moments when he was still alive for her.

Leah stared out the window at a strip of rosy sky wedged between treetops and black clouds. There was a density to the day, to the heavy salty air, that warned of rain or maybe snow showers. Maggie's scratching grew more frantic and she sighed, sat up, slid her feet into her shoes not bothering to change the socks she'd slept in, then pulled on sweatshirt and pants and made for the kitchen. It was what she'd wear all day. Doc always told her how pretty she looked; now it no longer mattered. She ran a brush through her hair, and in an childish fit of anger left the bed unmade, something she and Doc had sworn to never do, because both enjoyed plumped pillows, smoothed sheets, turned down blanket. The clock in the kitchen said five thirty. Maggie's tail thumped furiously as she ran back and forth between Leah and the front door, her eyes dark coals in the faint morning light.

"Okay," Leah said, her body lethargic, demanding coffee and more time to awaken. She put on her jacket and leaned over to leash Maggie. The dog's eyes swung to the bedroom and she began to whimper, suddenly refusing to move. Inhaling sharply with frustration, Leah jerked at the leash, pulling the dog to her side and opened the door.

Outside, the air was damp and chilled, trees motionless and glistening with moisture, sun buried behind a layer of grey clouds. The pearly gleam of a few minutes ago was gone. It was a cold New England morning rich with the dark scent of moist earth and pine needles. Crows cawed loudly overhead and settled into the oaks on the front lawn to watch her pass. The dog looked back at the closed door behind them. Leah felt a surge of anger and yanked hard on the leash again, immediately sorry at the dog's yelp. She took a deep breath.

"He's gone, Maggie," she said. "Can't you get that through your thick head?" She leaned down to scratch the dog behind the ears and whispered, "I'm sorry girl, for both of us."

Although early September, Doc had fired up the wood stove. Leah was grateful for the pungent smoky smell as she washed the dishes, enjoying the warm water running over her hands and the feel of the smooth wet surface of the china. Some memory of the crackling bark and deep rich smell of wood burning made Doc impatient for the first fire of the season, so that each year he lit it earlier than the year before. She imagined the first men crouched around a fire, holding back the night with its red-fingered warmth.

Something of that primordial sense of safety and comfort must exist in memory, easing the way into the cold and dark of winter. Foggy columns of smoke, visible, through the window over the sink, blew across the road and spiraled up over the pines until they were lost in a sky darkening into the early autumn night. She wrung out the sponge, wiped her hands on the dishtowel, hung it up and went to join him; the same routine most nights. After forty-two years of marriage, she'd been twenty-two when they married, Doc twenty-three, nothing was new, everything a ritual grown comfortable and reassuring.

Doc was in his chair, newspaper spread across his lap, a path of yellow light slicing his body from the floor lamp behind him. He'd moved her loom and the basket of wool closer to the stove as he did each autumn. Maggie lay stretched in front of him, one paw delicately resting over her muzzle, legs extended behind her and twitching in the midst of some dream. He smiled up at Leah, newspaper rustling as he shook it, prepared to offer her a section, and then all at once he stopped still, head cocked as though listening to something. A puzzled look passed over his face, and he put his hand over his chest, leaning back so that she saw his eyes fill with pain.

Doc said faintly, "Call the ambulance, Leah," then coughed and slid forward in the chair. She'd moved swiftly to help him, heart thumping wildly, and he whispered, "Now, Leah, call now," but something in his eyes was already drifting far away. The dog sprang up, lowering her head onto his knees, her eyes fixed on his face, hidden from Leah as his shoulders contracted and his head fell forward. Doc reached out, his fingers curling slowly over Maggie's skull as Leah dialed 911 and paced impatiently, shoulders rigid with fear. She stared out the window at leaves whipping through the air in a frenzied scarlet spiral as the autumn wind lifted them, listened for Doc's breathing, willing him to hold on.

"It's ringing," she said. "It'll be Okay." *Just a moment more,* she told herself, then, just as emergency services picked up, the dog began to howl, and she knew. She thought, then, that she must sink to the floor on all fours beside Maggie, the two of them with heads lifted to the unrelenting sky, howling in an ancient, visceral, frantic acknowledgement of death. Instead, with a steady voice, she answered, "My husband is having a heart attack," gave the address and asked them to hurry, even though the dog had told her there was no need.

They sat together beside Doc while they waited, the dog whimpering and Leah silent. She held Doc's hand in one of hers and smoothed back the thin white hair with the other, checking to be sure his shirt was clean and buttoned up, a last tribute to his sense of order.

The dog wouldn't eat. Every night Leah emptied out most of the food she'd put in Maggie's dish. She tried to tempt the dog by giving her the leftovers of her own untouched meals, but Maggie wouldn't even eat that, the same food she begged for during the whole thirteen years she'd been with them. It was as if the sole purpose of eating had been the nightly game of Doc slipping food to her under the table while Leah pretended she didn't notice.

"Not hungry?" She scratched the dog, smoothing the thick fur as Maggie looked up at her with dulled eyes. "Me neither."

The phone rang and she hesitated, not certain if she wanted to pick it up. It would be Ana's nightly call. If she didn't answer, Ana would be worried and probably drive over. She reached for the phone and felt that inexplicable sensation of falling she always felt at Ana's voice.

"Hi, what are you doing?" Then, as if Ana had witnessed the previous few minutes she said, "Maggie not eating yet."

"No." She hesitated then, with a catch in her voice, said "I guess neither one of us is very hungry."

Ana, always sensitive to Leah's moods after their fifty plus years of friendship, was silent a moment then asked, "Do you want me to come over for a while?"

Leah thought about Ana coming, silently noting the unmade bed, the clothes, the dark circles beneath her eye, and answered, "No. I was just about to put on some TV and I'll probably fall asleep in front of it. I'll see you tomorrow for lunch," cutting the conversation off.

Ana hesitated a moment then said, "Okay, see you then."

"Yes." Leah hung up.

Ana and Leah had been best friends since high school, crying together over boyfriends, bad grades, parental injustices, pimples, weight gains, celebrating all the rest. Ana had been with her when she met Doc. They were both in their last year of college and inspired by an unusually warm day, decided skip their class and picnic in a nearby park, transferring wine into a juice container and feeling very bold and reckless. Leah remembered, with a pang, how young they'd been, how sure of themselves. Doc, passing them on his way to a class, asked if he could join them and sat down without waiting for an answer. She'd taken it for granted that it was Ana he'd be interested in; Ana with her soft brown hair and long body, but he wasn't. He'd directed most of his attention to Leah and she liked the sound of his soft voice, something both magnetic and gentle about this man as he shared the history of the park and explaining that he wanted to work with plants in some way. There was a certain awkwardness about him, as though he wasn't sure he could pull this off, could make himself interesting enough to elicit a yes when he asked her for dinner that she found charming.

"Well," Ana said, when he walked away.   She brushed Leah's hair back from her face with tender fingers and Leah blushed.   "Now do you believe me when I tell you are every bit as pretty as I say you are."   Ana, to whom grades and dates came so effortlessly never failed to compliment Leah's intelligence, her long-lashed hazel eyes and the sweetness of her freckles, but Leah was never quite convinced.

Ana had been maid of honor at her wedding, staying over the night before, the two of them sharing wine, ridiculous jokes and memories from high school and college.   They'd gotten pretty drunk and Leah had fallen over onto the bed, whacking Ana on the way down leaving them both hysterical with laughter.   It had been then that what had seemed inevitable had finally happened, Ana kissed her, gently touching her face and hair.   Something had shattered inside Leah then, the breadth of something new and yet familiar, something utterly dangerous.   Leah returned the kiss, she couldn't help herself and then they began to unzip, unbutton, pull shirts over their heads, they couldn't stop, but Leah knew this was it, only this one time, only now.   The following morning neither had said anything, nor had either of them been embarrassed; something pent up and waiting had been given rein, and that freedom had somehow been enough.   A year later, Leah had been maid of honor at Ana and Joshua's wedding.

It was late-October, but whenever they began their walk, the dog turned and looked back toward the house, her ears pointed and listening for a voice she'd never hear again.   It was the same each morning, as if she now doubted her own baying pronouncement of Doc's death, only giving up once they were out of sight of the house.   Leah took the same route Doc always took, along the road that hugged the coast, despite the relentless wind. A squirrel clutching an acorn took to a tree at the sight of Maggie as they passed; turning to chatter angrily down at them, but the dog ignored it, nuzzling along the grass.   Leah turned onto the gravel road that ran along the rocky beach where the smooth red globes of rose hips hung from the stubby branches like Christmas ornaments.   The wind was brisker here and she felt salt spray on her lips as she stood watching the sun-glowing ocean. The white foam heads of waves reminded her of the curved backs of dolphins breaking the surface. It was low tide and seagulls dived crazily at water's edge, looking for clams and crabs exposed by the receding water.   One lifted a heavy clam and flew close to the ground, followed by a shrieking chorus of gulls attempting to steal it.   She laughed, and then picked her way over the sharp grey boulders.

The path dipped in a tight curve down around a dune and for a minute they were out of the wind and roar of the waves. All that was visible was the sky and thick green bushes and then the path rose up again and the ocean came slowly into view.   It was then that Leah saw the man coming toward them from the opposite end of the beach. His head was down against the wind.   His heavy plaid wool jacket and the cap he held tightly onto his head were like Doc's, a common occurrence in this part of Maine where most dressed for comfort.   One hand was jammed in his pocket and edges of thin gray hair peeked out over his ears.   The dog began to whine again, tugging frantically against the leash, tail fanning back and forth rapidly.   For a moment Leah's heart surged wildly as though the dog knew something she didn't, and she allowed Maggie to drag her along until they reached him.   He looked up, sparse hair blown around his cap like drying grass, offered a stranger's smile, said, "What a wind," then continued past them. Leah felt a sharp stab of disappointment that left her feeling angry and stupid.

"Foolish girl," she said to the dog whose tail sank between her legs, then bent to smooth the fur along her neck before they continued on their way.

The low respectful mummer of a crowd as Leah entered the funeral hall warned her of how many people had come to pay their respects to Doc. There were not only friends, but customers from the nursery, grateful to Doc for shoots and cuttings freely given, along with advice. She'd been a little dizzy at the fluorescent light and nauseous at the thickly sweet odor of the flowers everywhere, despite Leah's request for contributions to The Sierra Club instead; she supposed some people did both, but in the end it was probably fitting that he was surrounded with burst of color and leaves in death, since he'd been surrounded by them in life. She'd thought of taking Maggie with her left the house earlier in the day, dressed in Doc's favorite blue dress rather than the traditional black, a color he hated. The elderly dog came stiffly to her feet as if she'd read Leah's mind and stood looking at her, rigid and alert. Leah leaned over and cupped the dog's muzzle in her hands, certain the crowds would be too much for her. "I'll be home soon."

Ana had insisted she and Joshua would pick Leah up, but Leah had refused. She wanted to postpone the looks of compassion and symbols of support as long as possible. In truth, she wanted to mourn and bury Doc alone, closely holding her grief to her like a shawl. She brushed her hair noting how much chestnut still remained and applied a pale lipstick. Her eyes were shadowed with resignation, her face gaunt from the last few days when she'd only picked at her food. She sighed, grabbed the car keys, gave Maggie a final pat, put on the outside light, and left.

At the funeral home the name on the door of the room, Richard Willis White, momentarily confused her. She looked around for the right door, even thinking for one crazy moment that it was all a mistake and she could go home and find Doc sitting in his chair. He'd been called Doc for most of his adult life, because he could heal any ailing plant brought to Green Forays, the nursery he'd opened. Leah understood, then, that the same formality that announced a birth closed the circle at death. Doc was Richard Willis White again. She opened the door to a crowd already there and steeled herself to the hugs and commiserations of their friends. Ana, across the room, met her eyes over the small group around her and she felt comforted by the love she saw there.

Leah made her way to the open coffin and looked down, as she had yesterday by herself, into the face of a stranger. The stiff impassive features reflected none of the amiable intelligence and compassion that marked her husband, the mouth she remembered curved in kindness, was tight and crooked, the cheeks hollow. Death had obliterated Doc, replacing him with Richard Willis White, a different man than the one people had come to honor. Doc existed now only in the words she would hear from their friends, in the quick flashes of memory, like old movies they'd loved and would cease to exist they were gone. She didn't want others to see this stranger, to honor him as the man they'd known, that man was gone. She leaned over then and closed the coffin, struggling with the heavy lid, lowering it as quietly as possible, warning off the disconcerted director of the funeral parlor, holding one hand up in the air as he hastily stepped forward.

"It's Okay," she told him and then fumbled in her purse until she found a small photograph of Doc taken long ago that she always carried with her, and placed it on top of the coffin. He was speaking to a customer, smiling quizzically, his hand resting on the slender trunk of a mountain ash.

"I nearly brought Maggie," she whispered to Ana who came to sit beside her, holding her hand. *We're old now*, she thought, grateful that they settled into this profound relationship, those long ago feelings by now comfortable and treasured. Doc and Joshua had been the rock in both of their lives and neither of them regretted it. They'd seen each other nearly every day. Ana's two daughters regarded Leah as an aunt and she and Doc had taken them home for a week many times to allow Ana and Josh time alone.

"You should have brought her," Ana whispered.
Leah and Doc had never thought of getting a dog, not only were their lives too busy, but they were certain the pet would be considered a replacement for the children they'd never been able

to have. After her third miscarriage they'd decided enough, the hope and consequent sorrow was too much for them. They made their peace with being childless after a brief consideration of adopting, adored Ana's daughters, and their lives were good. But then, unexpectedly, there was Maggie. Doc had found her one night, abandoned in a dumpster, and with a tight face had brought her home, weak and dirty. Her matted fur smelling of rancid fruit had nauseated Leah. He'd gone right to the sink and put the whimpering puppy in and gently washed her, soaping the dirty fur and carefully cleaning her eyes.

"She can't be more than a month old," he said angrily, as he gently dried her.

Leah heated up some milk and crumpled bread and broke an egg into it. Later they'd fixed up a box, lining it with an old soft wool blanket, but the dog followed Doc to the bedroom and slept on the floor by his side of the bed. In the morning she was asleep on the bed by his feet, half-hidden under the blanket. From the beginning Maggie was Doc's dog. She waited for him at the door every night, protesting when Leah tried to take her out for a walk, so that even with pneumonia, Doc had gotten up, despite Leah's protests, to take her out for her regular walk along the beach.

After their morning walk, Leah put on the kettle for tea and offered Maggie a dog treat, but the dog ignored it, settling into the place in front of the door where she'd spent nearly every waking moment since Doc's death, her nose resting on her paws, her tail unmoving. Leah shook her head. "You've got to accept it, girl," she said to the dog. The kettle whistled and she made herself a mug of blackberry tea with honey, and turned, mug in hand, to her loom. She'd taken an order for ten shawls to be delivered by Thanksgiving that she should work on, but instead, seeing the envelopes strewn over the table, she decided to answer the cards she'd received in the mail and pulled from the flowers sent by friends to the funeral home. She sat down, cup of tea in front of her, and reached for the pen.

You're old, Leah told herself, as she realized she'd drifted off again, and turned her attention back to the table. There must have been a hundred cards and notes. She wrote, folded, addressed and stamped the envelopes until she was almost finished. All at once she recognized by the light it was late afternoon. Massaging her hand and twisting her shoulders as she sealed one of the last envelopes, she absently called, "Doc, would you bring me a glass of water?" The dog was immediately on her feet, whining, and Leah, felt a welling-up inside her.

"Stop," she told the dog in a choked voice and stood up to get something to drink. She looked at her reflection in the window over the sink; "Get over it," she told herself angrily

Leah stopped walking Maggie along the beach, going instead through the near-by woods. It had been a warm autumn, their favorite season, this period between summer and winter when everything seemed to stand still for a brief period and hold its breath and despite it being November the vivid colors had lingered. Geese flew honking overhead, black V's in long geometric formations against a flat blue sky and drifting clouds. Coppery bracken ferns, long gold pine needles fallen over the muddy path, comforting smell of sweet-fern, and blazing trees arching against a restless sky made her ache with longing, sending her hurrying back to her weaving. She'd accepted far more orders than she could reasonably fill, but she was grateful to be busy.

A few days later, when Leah was lost in the meditative monotony of throwing a shuttle, working the treadles rhythmically with her feet, Maggie leaped up suddenly and stood pawing the door. It was growing dark and Leah realized that she'd skipped lunch again. The dog was keening softly and Leah sat staring at her, confused by her sudden agitation. Then she heard footsteps on the sidewalk outside, and recognized something familiar in the cadence of the stride.   Her stomach churned and she felt faint. The dog was pacing frantically now, whining sharply, twisting back and forth between door and Leah as the footsteps grew closer.

Did they pause? " Doc?" Leah whispered, then the footsteps went past the gate and Maggie sank suddenly to the floor with a whimper.   Leah swallowed hard, closing her eyes tightly against the tears that threatened, and for a second rested her forehead against a trembling hand, then turned to the dog who lay motionless now. "Dumb, dumb, dumb," she hissed, suddenly angry, "He's dead. Grow up."

The final week of November, she woke to frost coating the window. The sun through the silver-etched glass was bright and birds fluttered rapidly around the feeder in a storm of colored feathers and piercing cries.   The thermometer said twenty-eight degrees and the grass was white crystal that crackled as she and Maggie walked through the woods, taking care not to slip on the icy leaves carpeting the ground. Overhead the thick clouds covering the sun glowed like the dying embers of a fire.

Ana called that day as she'd done every Saturday to ask how Leah was and if she was sleeping and if she should come over.

"Yes, I'm sleeping" Leah brusquely lied, not wanting to reveal the troubled short bursts of sleeping and waking she experienced through a long dark night.   She was afraid to see Ana too often, afraid that some dam of strength she'd built around Doc's death would burst and there'd be no way to live with the sorrow.

Something in her voice alerted Ana. "You could speak to the doctor about taking something if you are having a problem," she suggested. "It's natural to have a problem sleeping after somebody you've lived with for forty-eight years dies."

"Dying is natural, too and we should be used to it by our age," Leah snapped. A knot at the base of her stomach moved up until her chest felt as though it would explode. She swallowed hard, and apologized.

"And Maggie?"

"She hasn't got it through her head yet that he's gone. She keeps leaping up at every sound," she said and thought of the footsteps outside the door, coming closer, then away, thought of her own heart leaping up at the sight of the man on the beach. "It'll probably be till winter stuck in the house, just the two of us, when she finally accepts it."

"It takes time, Leah," Ana said and hearing the sympathy in her friend's voice Leah found an excuse to quickly hang up.

The house, now, seemed that of a stranger's, each room familiar, yet lacking familiarity. Never had she lived there alone and each item, the wood carrier by the stove, the dishes shiny with the patina of use through her and Doc's long marriage, the chair with the indentation still of his weight, all seemed things she knew but that belonged to somebody else. It was almost as though the very air had been pulled out of each room. Often, she felt smothered and peculiarly breathless and buried herself in her weaving. She heard her voice, as she wove, absent-mindedly speaking with him the way she used to, discussing the color and textures of the wool, the price that she paid, who the order was going to, and needed to bring herself up short with remembering. And each time she said his name Maggie would spring up, nose against the door, duplicating her own merciful memory lapse.

As Christmas drew near, Ana grew persistent that Leah and Maggie come Christmas Eve and stay overnight, but Leah put her friend off. It was as though leaving the house would be a betrayal, almost as though she needed to be there in case he returned.   She shook her head again and again to clear it of this nonsense.

The week before Christmas a snowstorm blew in full and fast from the north during the night, the wind waking her as it hammered the wet flakes fiercely against the window. Leah snuggled down deeply into the blankets, feeling the deep cold of winter that had invaded the room and wished that she'd lit the wood stove the night before, a job Doc had claimed. He loved piling the kindling over old newspaper, making the small teepee of thinly split logs, striking the match and watching the red flames leap up in the sudden rush of crackling fire devouring the wood.   She hadn't gotten around to firing up the stove since his death, relying on the oil heat instead.

Maggie began to whimper frantically, her body trembling as she raised up on hind legs and pushed her nose against the drapes trying to part them.   Leah listened closely and through the howling wind she thought she could hear a vague whistling, high and sharp. She felt a chill course through her that the warmth of the blankets couldn't dispel.

"It's the wind," she muttered to the dog, but Maggie wouldn't be quiet, wouldn't fall back to the hooked rug she'd slept on since Doc died.   She howled then a strange eerie cry so high and peculiar that Leah felt a sudden tug of fear.

"There's nobody out there, Maggie," she said, listening to the wildly blowing cold wind. *Nobody could tolerate that swirling white mass for long,* she thought, and then, *what are you thinking?* "What is it Maggie?" she asked and despite herself felt an explosive burst of hope that she couldn't understand, unreasonable but dauntless in its insistence.

"Okay," she whispered and stood up, pulling her shawl around her against the sharp bite of the winter air. She crossed the braided rug slowly to the window, chiding herself the whole time for what she was doing. The room was dark; she'd pulled the drapes tight against the night, and she felt like a child lost in a grown-up's world. The dog turned and pushed herself against Leah, insistently begging, then stretched up again, paws on the windowsill, nose tucked between the drapes. Leah took a deep breath, whispering in a voice she didn't recognize, "Doc?" and with a trembling hand flung the drapes open and screamed, although there was nothing but white fists of snow smashing against the window and desperate tree branches like dark arms blowing in a thick curtain of movement that took her breath away.

She caught her breath, her heart pounding painfully in her chest and began to tremble uncontrollably. She looked down at the dog, standing quietly now beside her leg. There was a strange luminous glow from the pale snow-filled night outside the window and the heavy plaid wool blankets on the bed were clearly illuminated.

"He's dead, Maggie. He's dead," she said and some waiting anticipation that she hadn't realized she felt, that had filled the hollowness of his absence was suddenly gone and she felt for a moment as though she was floating, looking down at her bed at the braided rug, the worn rocking chair and then she drifted back into herself and the room was suddenly familiar for the first time in months. She felt calmer, despite the tension that lingered in her body. The dog, after a moment, leaped onto the foot of the bed, circled in the blanket and was still. Leah felt the fluttering inside her refuse to quiet, although her mind seemed still and exact, and thought of making a cup of tea or lighting the wood stove. Instead, aware of a profound weariness, she climbed beneath the covers and listened to the storm violently flooding the night, watching the shifting white night through the window.

The next morning Leah woke all at once to the dog's nails scratching at the door. Silence had fallen with the snow all around the house and it seemed to Leah as if the world had stopped breathing. She realized that she hadn't pulled the drapes closed and strong clear sunlight tinged with blue filled the room.

"All right, all right," she told Maggie, "I'm coming." She stood shivering in the still, cold air, and looked out. Branches were heavy with snow, tiny green points of needles poking through. The tracks of birds and squirrels hatch-marked the white like the stitching of a quilt. The overhead sky was palely frosted, ground hidden, and everywhere nothing but white. There must have been eight inches at least. She'd have to snow-blow after she walked the dog. She put the kettle on and made herself a cup of coffee, telling Maggie she'd have to wait. Then she dragged on heavy wool pants, a flannel shirt and thick sweater, two pairs of socks and her boots.

Drinking the coffee she thought about building a fire and assessed the wood piled before the stove. She decided to haul in at least two more loads when they came back. She realized that the snow would be too soft and deep in the woods now, and perhaps for the rest of the winter, to walk her there and decided to take the path leading to the water. Maggie followed her around the kitchen whining urgently and Leah soothed her as she got ready. She put a wind-breaker on, then her mittens and took the leash down, prepared for the usual struggle with the dog, but Maggie ran to the door immediately and looked up at her without looking behind. As soon as Leah snapped the leash on, Maggie was pushing at the door, eager to go.

Leah slowly turned to the bedroom and looked at the unmade bed and the drapes flung wide, but the dog was anxious and pulled at her arm. A heaviness that made it hard to breathe hammered at her chest then gave way little by little, till it finally collapsed under the weight of itself, and she accepted the truth of the coming winter; the streets and highways iced over and sometimes impassable, that truth of being left forever without him.

Her love for Doc that informed each breath she took, would, on each breath's exhale, disperse through the large empty house till the rooms were flooded, loss but also love reverberating endlessly, an echo that she would never stop hearing. She looked out the frozen window at the world, colorless and buried in the avalanche of snow.

She leashed Maggie who began tugging; pulling her forward and she opened the door, knowing it was time to move on.

55.
To Grandma's House
John J. Brugaletta

We wished for this, back in the summer's heat,
the innocence with which the snow blankets
shrubs, abandoned toys, forgotten wrenches.

It has been long enough since last winter
so that icicles on holiday cards are charming again,
though the real ones betray a lack of insulation.

Now we have our wish. (We always have.):
The outdoor breaths that numb our lungs,
and black ice on country roads, beyond which

grandparents wait a special dinner for us,
hoping we haven't slid into a ditch,
but never saying a word about their fears.

The joyful mien of course is meant to cover
the awful fact that winter is the season of death,
despite the smiles and the anachronistic greenery.

56.
Windy City
Mark Hudson

On a windy day
A man crossed the street
The wind blew his hat off
While a car approached him
He didn't lose his smile
And picked up the hat
And put it back on his head
And went about his business

57.
Winter Dawn
Yasmin Khan

icy clouds nudged by sun~~
a grey dawn....
warmth of quilts~~
as wind howls in the trees....
a cold wave sweeps across~~
life stands still....

58.
Winter Moon
Cate Caldwell

This time of year, so much is silver. The moon glitters off the ice and snow, eye watering bright. And me, I am silver. When I look down, antlers heavier and heavier, I see my chest and forelegs have become silver, too. But still I am venerable.

I bring my hoof, sharp in the winter, down hard on the ice. It cracks, allowing me to get to the lichen underneath. It's good to eat in the frozen time.

We are strong and we are many, though not as many now as in summer. The young ones start families. We split into smaller groups when the nights became longer, and begin the long run to the forest. It's the best place to find food during the night season. It is good to run. During autumn, our hooves pound on the softer ground, blood pumping through our veins. We outrun many things, sometimes even the growling bugs with round legs that only run on the black river-like meadows. I am always a little sorry when the long run is over.

Now, the young ones fight. They rise up, antlers clashing under the indigo sky, to test which of them is the bravest. I was there, too, not long ago. One looks up as if to issue a challenge. I glare moodily under my antlers, which are almost as tall as he is. He prances off.

I chew my lichen and watch the strangers. Tiny creatures, most of them, some with long ears, some with fluffy tails, all worried about finding food. The big roaring ones with sharp claws have mostly gone to sleep. Then the howling begins.

This one's name I know: Wolf.

The young ones gaze about, dancing from side-to-side. They wonder whether to be afraid. I lock eyes with one of them, a big one. His eyes are silver. His fur is also, but unlike mine, his has always been so. He is not very big, less than a third of my size, but his teeth are sharp. And he is hungry. But my horns are sharp, too, I think. And I want to live.

Perhaps someday you will bring me down, wolf. But not today.

Others of their pack gather on the hill. They pace, proudly lifting their faces toward the moon. They erupt into their war cry, a throaty howl that says, "We are wolves!" And they thunder down the hill.

I stand my ground. I know that I must. I have seen too many of my brethren fall. They fell because, spooked, they turned and fled. Hindquarters thus exposed, the old and the sick fell behind and became easy to pull into the snow.

But head on, the wolves will not risk the horns. We are too large, and too many. And they do not want to risk a crippling wound that will prevent them from hunting. We all know that a wound can mean we will not see the next spring.

They leave, disappointed. They must find other prey, today. Smaller prey. I am glad I must only dig for lichen.

A green and pink glow is splashed across the horizon. Life is good.

As the winter goes on, there is not enough lichen for all. When I look at my fellows, I see ribs through many of their coats. Some of the females, with child, are starting to show. They should be eating more, not less. How many of us will make it to spring?

I am not as hale as I once was.   I feel an ache in my joints and a stabbing pain in my side when I first wake.   The young ones treat me like an elder.   They seem concerned.   I try to reassure them that it will be better soon, that it is almost spring.   But this winter is very long.

After many weeks, I see my friend the wolf.   He's skinnier than before, with sharper, more desperate eyes.   His eyes reflect the desperation in those of my brethren.   Their eyes say, will there be enough food for all? Will we make it until spring?

The wolves begin their chant, bolstering each other's pride and courage.   When they charge down the hill, I let myself fall behind.   Then, I turn and I flee.

59.
Winter
Michelle Cacho-Negrete

Winter blasts us with four blizzards nearly back-to-back. Snow explodes - avalanches tumbling from a sullen sky. By mid-afternoon, opaque waves of white render every other color obsolete: a sort of snow-blindness. Swift sheets of wind shape fleeing ghosts that haunt corners and circle trees. The snow provides its own brightness, sucking up residual sunlight and beaming it back to us like a flat, cold sun.

We're prepared: split wood columned beside the woodstove, a can of maple syrup for sugar on snow, flashlights in every room. Kevin, my husband, has a stack of New Yorker Magazines. I am reading a book on the Inuit, a culture inseparable from, and reliant upon, winter. The Inuit word for winter is *ukivq*, which is also the word for year and the long Maine winter can indeed feel like a year. The Inuit consider extreme conditions and the lengthy absence of daylight a time for dreaming, storytelling, communicating with the spirits, as if the distraction of sunlight obfuscates clarity. It is an enviable purity similar to the Buddhist philosophy of seeing the world as it is and finding the joy in it.

The fire crackles, spits sparks of red and blue, the air redolent with burning wood. Our house, a warm cave carved into the cold, has grown a shell of snow. I rest my fingers against the flake-dusted window that reflects my transparent face, turbulence whirling behind it as though some spirit wind moves though me. Pines jitterbug to a fierce melody. Chickadees dart at birdfeeders then soar away as though snatched by the wind. I remove my fingers from the glass, their frosty shape gradually fading like an old photograph in too much light.

There is never a day that we don't go out. The Inuit word, Sila, roughly translates as the breath of the world, consciousness, weather and so much more. Kevin and I need Sila, need that breath. In late afternoon, we dress in snowsuits, strap on snowshoes, battle the wind for control of the door and go out. A merciless gust steals my breath. Stiffness seizes me as though my limbs are frozen. The air vibrates, a wind instrument playing a tuneless scale. We shoe across the backyard into the woods where we're sheltered by pine and hemlock, branches bowed beneath the snowy weight. The orange flagging Kevin tied to individual trees to mark a path is hidden by snow that has caterpillared up tree trunks. We look for landmarks, but there has been a shift, the familiar and unfamiliar residing in each other. We have been relocated to a country of ephemera: growing mounds of snowdrifts, miniature hills birthing on tree boughs, newly recorded animal markings that vanish even as we watch. Kevin brushes tree-trunks with a gloved hand, seeking flags with little success and we concentrate, instead, on plowing through the white world around us.

Thick layers cover our boots and threaten the theft of our snowshoes, our journey narrated by snowshoe tracks splayed out behind us. Just as birds ate Hansel and Gretel's breadcrumbs, the falling snow will eat our tracks. I scale rising drifts by grasping tree trunks, quickly drenched with perspiration beneath my jacket and snowpants. Even my fingers and toes, originally protesting the ten-degree temperature with numbness, are comfortable.

There is a joke in Maine; if you don't like the weather, wait five minutes, but this year's contrasts have been startling. The preceding week brought fifty to fifty-five degree temperatures, broke weather records and deposited a false patina of spring. Kevin and I strolled nearby Ogunquit, a tourist town mostly shuttered in winter. Visitors, giddy in the January thaw, bought hot chocolate and donuts from one of the few open shops. Kevin, a research scientist whose work involves trees and global climate change, paused to examine prematurely spouting pussy willows, those furry precursors of spring.

"Nearly two months early," he said, running his fingers over the buds.

The willows were not alone in their confusion as to what season it was: oak and maple buds were swelling, the sharp tips of daffodils poking through layers of slushy ice. We walked between two closed hotels to reach Marginal Way, a cliff walk mobbed with natives taking advantage of the warmth, a few teenagers in Bermuda shorts, most of us wearing sneakers rather than boots. Strangers greeted each other with "Beautiful day." The cliff path winding along the ocean was alternately puddled or icy as snow from the previous week had repetitively melted and froze. We'd all regressed to clumsy toddlers as we gingerly navigated patches of ice. The ocean smacked the cliffs with thick veils of white foam as waves lifted and dropped with unrestrained power. The sky was the flat blue of blown glass and temporarily cloudless. I understood the perils of global climate change, yet couldn't help feeling energized after a week of shrouded skies, perleroneg, the sense of being crazed by extended darkness, vanquished.

The sun's rose-tinged descent by four o'clock seemed incongruous with the spring weather, as though the warmth could somehow extend daylight. We headed home, reluctant to let go of the day. Our son called just as we got there, told us about taking his daughters, two-year-old Sadie and four-year-old Ceiligh, out to the park near his house. I spoke briefly to each as they informed me, with some sadness that their snowman had melted. I told them that the opportunity to build other snowman was likely. The following morning the temperature dropped sharply and snow pounded us as though revenging the warmth of the previous days.

Those soaring temperatures had encouraged the formation of vernal pools in our woods way ahead of their traditional spring arrival. The Inuit call spring *immaturpuq*, "when the Earth receives its first water," and vernal pools, "the first water" are spring's welcome harbingers, amoebic-like sacs of snowmelt that nourish various species from infancy to adulthood.   We struggled to avoid stepping into these thinly iced bowls even as they sucked snow down their sides like quicksand, splitting the ground into snaking ditches.   Again and again we encountered narrow streams widening into miniature lakes, sometimes plunging into them as the snow caved beneath our feet.

There seemed a literary quality to this juxtaposition of winter and spring crammed together, how the fiery heat of snow against my cheeks echoed July sun, a reminder of the smooth flow of the seasons.   I marveled at how nature had perfected a continuum carefully balanced to sustain life, each season's process one of death and rebirth: spring laboriously conquering winter, summer's abundance running rampant over spring, autumn's blazing take-down of summer, winter's shortened days forcing life underground, then the expanding light of spring renewing the cycle. Kevin and I have watched the growing disruptions with dismay. Autumnal breaks in summer with forty-degree weather that incites premature senescence in trees; spring-like fissures in winter, rising temperatures waking buds that will freeze in the plunge back to frigidity; seasonal havoc occurring more frequently and more intensely each passing year.

Late afternoon's last gasping bursts of ivory heralded the end of the latest storm. The yard was a pale lunarscape that ran into the darkness of the woods. The austerity of this rippled white deepened the greened density just beyond. The rising boulders of our ancient granite quarry had morphed into a sprawl of something softer, rounder. Winter in Maine is not just a season but a location, sign-posted in layers of cold-white drifts and gritty ice.

Kevin went outside to snow-blow the driveway while I raked the roof of the woodshed beside our buried deck, the raked snow contributing to the mountain that made roof and deck a single level. When I was done, I sat on the snow-mountain and admired the variegated shades of soft gray that quilted the sky. The cold was so intense that breathing seemed an aerobic activity, yet peace had taken hold.   The wind had stopped its moaning and quiet was its own sound, although it's never really quiet. There's the rapid run of a squirrel up a tree, the flap of chickadees at the birdfeeder, the marauding wind through the spruce and pine.   Once when I visited a friend in central Maine who lived near a frozen lake, we listened to the ringing, humming, groaning of cracking ice as the afternoon passed.

"The Earth speaking," he told me with glowing face; remembering that I think, *Sila*.

By the time Kevin and I went inside to eat dinner, it was fully dark. Clouds obfuscated evening light, landscape indistinct in the absence of moon and stars.   This blurry vista, sometimes occurring after a blizzard, has always appeared apocalyptic to me, a reminder of how fragile and yet resilient everything is and of how carelessly we challenge that resilience.

I looked out at the camouflaging layers, knowing there would be more to come. Snow sometimes remains on the ground well into spring.   One May I flew home from California and looked down at a patchwork of white, green and brown. That lingering snow is one reason winter feels a year long, yet snow is vital to the ecology of Maine, indeed to all snow-laden areas.   It is a blanket that insulates life germinating underground.   The year we had little snow and frigid temperatures, half our garden plants didn't return, crops suffered, and there was a shortage of food for migrating birds.
 In the middle of the night I was woken by wind that had returned with renewed ferocity.   It circled the house like a growling dog.   I opened my eyes to an incandescent glow; the room's contents hued in hazy silver.   It was cold, the wood stove long out, and I shivered as I walked to the window, which framed a startlingly bright full moon, the snow beneath it a spill of soft opalescence. Shadows crept across the yard like scurrying animals as the wind

seized everything it could. Oaks and maples, reduced to their essential skeletons in winter, were bathed in pearled-white. Fleeing clouds scrolled a manuscript of sharp white stars out behind them. An owl flew by, its shadow looming over a scurrying rodent that vanished behind the snowbound rock wall. The deep moans of the wind seeped in as if by osmosis.   Wind and trees engaged in a battle of strength as the wind furiously shook the trees.   I knew that by daylight a few would not have survived the assault.

The temperature the next morning was minus four and the air seemed fragile as crystal, as if it might shatter from the mere act of moving through it.   The sun shed pale gold over the trees, their shadows wavering columns across the yard. The radio spoke of unusually cold air. I pulled on a heavy sweater, lined jeans, and wool socks then went downstairs. Kevin, awake earlier than usual, had lit the wood stove and made coffee.   As I poured myself a cup he opened the door, bundled in high boots, thick jacket, pants over thermal underwear. His eyes were watery, nose red, boots crusted with snow.   He pulled off his gloves, flexed his fingers then cupped them around a cup of coffee I handed him.

"I have to leave for work in a minute, I just wanted to see what fell last night; mostly softwoods. We may have to cut an oak for next winter if one doesn't come down over the next few months."

Next winter, I thought, *we're still in the middle of this one.* But then, sometimes winter seems the only season, briefly punctuated by warmth. We prepare for it no matter where we are in the calendar. After a blizzard, Kevin chainsaws downed trees we'll use for the following winter. Once snow melts in late spring, we pile them onto our wheelbarrow and pull them to an old oak stump where he'll split each log. Through summer and autumn, Kevin splits wood that we haul and stack in the woodshed. We gather branches and twigs for kindling, buy mulch to cover plants, repair storm windows damaged by rodents or rot, check ice scrapers, snow blowers, heaters. I don't want to plan for next winter in the midst of this one, but I'm already mulling over next year as though time has fast-forwarded.

Kevin kisses me goodbye, his car vanishing behind snow corridors piled high along the road by the snowplow. I stare out at the sprawling terrain and the house grows cramped. I eat a bowl of oatmeal as I watch birds swoop and dip into the pool of water created by our sump pump, then leave my dish in the sink, pull on mittens, jacket and snowshoes and slide down the slope of snow-curved steps. My face stings. My toes complain. My breath fans out behind me so thickly that I imagine it a contrail too dense to evaporate. I shoe into the woods striped by thin ribbons of light that christen treetops with brightness and offer a broken path of radiance. Everything shimmers, a thousand shafts of sun like a fire in the snow. I pass between trees as if through doorways, slide down small hills, find my way around the vernal pools packed with leaves and lichen-dressed twigs pressed beneath ice like cloudy glass. I kneel to peer in at a complicated sculpture of lacy green lichen, rough brown twigs, curling russet leaves, white birch bark. The sun moves overhead and my shadow is suddenly part of the sculpture, reminding me that in some Inuit dialects, the word for man is interchangeable with the word for shadow.

There is an Inuit word, *ablautseneq*: corporeal and perceptual transformation. Traditional Inuit believed that a shaman could shape-shift into any animal, described in the poem Magic Words: "Sometimes they were people, and sometimes animal, and there was no difference. They all spoke the same language." In Western culture, that concept is alien, but here in the woods I want to believe in the possibility; I want to be a fox I once saw flying across the snow. I stand and begin to shoe again. An earlier history has been written beneath my feet on snow parchment; bird, deer, domestic cats, dogs and coyote tracks. My own, created by wide, multi-squared plastic, dissolve any fantasy of *ablautseneq*; I am only a middle-aged, American white woman.

I have become so immersed in my musings that I paid no attention to last night's faint snowshoe tracks and find myself lost. I am no more than five or six acres from a house or road in any direction yet feel, for one moment, panic, a vestigial reflex from a time before we'd converted most wilderness into subdivided house plots, before industrialization began to separate us from the natural world, homogenizing everything into a bland comfort, pumping out greenhouse gases that may one day render winter obsolete.   A puff of woodsmoke blows toward me and I move in its direction, sniffing the air like a wild dog, till I'm in my backyard. Later, I share the story with my son Carl who says, "Okay, no grandkids wandering in the backyard alone."

By February, mid-winter, a deep cold sets in. Kevin and I dress in so many layers to go out we feel like mummies. The wind is frequently biting, black ice everywhere, walking treacherous, but we go outside; breathe with the world, center consciousness, sila, as winter wraps that world with its frosty breath of life, and offer thanks, hope for its continuance.   We hear, more frequently now, meteorologists speak about unseasonable cold here, unseasonable heat elsewhere, droughts, monsoons, mudslides. Inuit believe shaman on mystical journeys accept responsibility to atone for tribal transgressions and to restore balance in the everyday world. Outside in the dwindling light, amid skeletons of oak and maple, I mourn for our children and grandchildren, forced to take on that responsibility, atoning to the planet for the ways their forebearers have mistreated it.

By February's end, I yearn for brightness to lengthen days, become an expanding highway between shortening nights. Each winter, incremental increases of daylight after solstice are so gradual that I don't experience them, until one morning everything seems to explode into light. I envy the Inuit firmly centered in the cold, mystical qualities of a world with intermittent light. I resolve to work harder, to make these short days more productive, to further appreciate the austere, sculptural beauty of the winter landscape, to fully nourish myself with darkness, to live in the present moment.

As if to taunt me for my resolve, two days of fifty-five degree weather appear. Ice melts from the roof, a sparkling mini waterfall. Conifers seem to suck up green from the air. Black dots, stark against the hard-packed snow, come to life; snow fleas, also called springtails. These tiny insects, beckoned from their dormancy by the late-April-like weather, frolic wildly echoing my own intoxication with the unnatural warmth despite knowing that this is global climate change puncturing holes in the natural order of things. I reread an Inuit poem: "Oh how entrancing, oh how joyful, I lay me on the ground sobbing." Over the next few days temperatures dropped to twenty, rose, and fell again.

I drive to Massachusetts to meet Carl and my granddaughters the following week, on a forty-five degree day of bright sunlight. We are spending the afternoon at Parker River Refuge on Plum Island, a natural barrier island of 4,662 acres of dunes, beaches, salt marshes, mini-forests of thickets and shrubs. When I arrive at his house the snow is branded, as it is in all cities, with streaky car exhaust, muddy footprints, debris; sun transforming it into speckled cornices of ice. However, on the shady boardwalks winding through the refuge, snow has retained some pristine element. Bright gold slits through the mixed canopy overhead, fires snow like flecks of mica, mantles this natural world with an enticing sheen. My granddaughters want to hold it. They pull off their mittens, cup mounts of snow in their hands, watch it melt, wipe their dripping palms against their jackets, then repeat the process, oblivious to their chilled fingers.

The boardwalk is surrounded by phragmites, a sixteen-foot grass with feathery, waving tops. Rhizomes, their underground hollow stems, need little to careen across marshes and this invasive species has taken over completely but their thousands of plumes fanning the air is magnificent. We break off a stem for each girl. They march along the boardwalk waving these furry flags which tower over them.

Later, we walk out to the banks where the Parker River mirrors the fiery globe of the setting sun. Life flourishes here, in the depth of winter. Ducks swim in iridescent groups, webbed feet paddling like battery-powered toys. A northern harrier surveys its territory, a moment later soaring into the air, silhouetted against the sky. I think, for a moment, it's after a duck, but perhaps discouraged by the density of these quacking water-clowns, it flies in the opposite direction. My granddaughters are charmed by a flock of red-necked grebes, heads bobbing underwater, tails wagging in the air.

Temperatures lower in the shift from afternoon to evening, and scrub oaks shiver in a rising wind. After the unseasonable warmth of the day, the twenty-or-so-degrees is sharply cutting.

"Cold," Sadie says. We nod agreement.

"Cold," Carl repeats. "Time to go home."

As we turn up the path to our car, Ceiligh points and says, "Look, the moon and the sun at the same time."

As we stare, a dense cloud of starlings appears; their dark sheen and white spots paled by the lowering light, their peculiar vocalizations drifting through the air. As if to impress us, they execute the most precise, perfect series of swoops, darts, turns; aerial creatures of such grace that we are mesmerized by their pirouettes against a backdrop of purpling sky.

"Dancing birds," Sadie says laughing and applauding. My granddaughters watch the ballet overhead and then Ceiligh throws her arms open, begins to slowly twirl and a moment later to sing, her small voice blending with the quacks, flapping and overhead cries. Her spontaneous song seems a part of the river, the birds, the trees. She sings out loud her relationship with the Earth.   The Inuit poet-shaman Orpingalik said, "Songs are thoughts, sung out with the breath when people are moved by great forces and ordinary speech no longer suffices…. All my being is songs and I sing as I draw breath."

A moment later, Sadie emulates her older sister, and begins to sing and spin also; two tiny dervishes, arms stretched wide to welcome the winter night.

Ceiligh sings, "I love snow. I love the moon."

Sadie chimes in with, "Love, snow, moon."

Ceilgh's song is a chant, rhythmic and hypnotic and in the descending darkness, she and Sadie are part of winter's kaleidoscope. My granddaughters are dreaming, traveling on their own mystical journey, flowing into the coldness and fading light without fear or reservation. Watching them stirs old memories of once being a child who welcomed each snowfall that draped my Brooklyn Ghetto in mystery. I blew breath again and again to marvel at the white mist, sat on my fire-escape nearly every night, swaddled in layers of clothes and blanket, thrilled by the early darkness that revealed winter constellations swirling overhead.

I recently read a report stating spring now arrives fifteen to twenty-four days earlier, disrupting the patterns of migrant birds, growing plants, insects.   I fear it swallowing more and more of the life-sustaining days of winter, of snow melting for the last time, leaving behind a different world: the sharp winter stars of Pegasus soaring over a sorrowful, scorched landscape. It seems to me that what I want is small, yet immense; that generations of children will hear the wind hum through winter trees, will compose songs of snow and moon, will witness the geometric sketching of animal and bird tracks over white frigid fields.

Just as we reach our car, great flakes of white begin to tumble around us; rain transformed to a state of grace. We pause, four tiny promontories of this vast Earth we are joined to. The sun, as it slips into the dark envelope of night, imbues the falling white with a final luminous radiance. The whisper of snow takes over the evening. We stand quietly then, breathing in, breathing out, breathing in unison with the Earth.

60.
Winter's Blanket
Yasmin Khan

a gilded gliding
lily white, gossamer light~~
snowflake confetti

tumbling down gently
pristine delicate crystals~~
sedate, coquettish

a virgin embrace
enveloping the landscape~~
a silver garnish

Contributing Authors

A.J. Huffman

A.J. Huffman

Where are you from?
Ormond Beach, Florida

When and why did you begin writing?
Writing always just kind of came naturally to me. I wrote my first short story in grade school. It was about living in a yellow submarine with my pet fish. And I, of course, I wrote poetry in high school. But I didn't actually start taking my writing seriously until I got to college.

What would you say is your most interesting writing quirk?
I still prefer to write with a pen on paper. My writing friends think I'm nuts. They are all die-hard type straight to the screen computer writers.

What do you like to do when you're not writing?
Dude! I live in Florida! I'm at the beach!

As a child, what did you want to do when you grew up?
When I was a little girl I wanted to be a fashion designer. I was a total girly girl. I loved clothes and dresses and shoes. Oh wait, I still do, I just can't sew.

Austin VanKirk

A. D. VanKirk

Where are you from?
I am from Petersburg, Michigan, which is only a short hike to
Toledo, Ohio. This setting was used in my
Short story, "Home for the Holidays"

When and why did you begin writing?
I began writing when I was six years old. I was in the first grade at
time, and to improve our reading skills, my teacher asked us to read
these small children's books. I found them incredibly dull, and
Decided that I would write and illustrate my own with the help of
my mother.

What would you say is your most interesting writing quirk?
My writing quirks aren't terribly interesting to most, but if pressed
I'd say that I write while listening to music. I find it stimulating and
my keystrokes usually sync up with the songs' beat.

What do you like to do when you're not writing?
I'm a big fan of naps. I also enjoy playing certain video games that
have inspiring storylines.

As a child, what did you want to do when you grew up?
As a child, I wanted to be many things: a professional soccer player,
a lawyer, a detective—the list is rather long. I grew and changed
much, and now am finding myself a writer and editor.

Cate Caldwell

Cate Caldwell

Where are you from?
Detroit, MI

When and why did you begin writing?
I've been writing since I could hold a pencil. I began binding my own books in kindergarten and won the young author's contest in first grade.

What would you say is your most interesting writing quirk?
I have a meditation I do before writing which involves candles, creative visualization, an 'increase your creativity' recording and a short prayer.

What do you like to do when you're not writing?
Hiking, camping and scuba diving. Also, reading and watching good theater.

As a child, what did you want to do when you grew up?
I've always wanted to be a writer! But when I was really little I wanted my own variety show like Sonny and Cher. Which tells you something about my age.

Deborah Guzzi

Deborah Guzzi

Where are you from?
I've lived predominantly on the east coast of the USA from Maine to Maryland.

When and why did you begin writing?
I began writing after a traumatic experience in high school.

What do you like to do when you're not writing?
Read, hike, kayak.

As a child, what did you want to do when you grew up?
Teach.

School's Out first appeared in the January 2014 online issue of *Contemporary Haibun*, Online vol. 9 number 4.

Earl W. Wolfe

Earl W. Wolfe

Where are you from?
Born and raised in Detroit. Schooled in engineering, then exposed to research, rockets, airplanes, cars, tractors, big trucks and pickups before retiring.

When and why did you begin writing?
Product engineering and research are essentially exercises in communication. Verbal and written directions plus necessary reports and letters were essential parts of my work. Unfortunately, an over-active sense of humor resulted in the recording of my observations of the fun in life on paper. I showed examples of my work to several who became my ex-friends.

What would you say is your most interesting writing quirk?
I love whimsy and sardonic whimsy, and I have no reservations recording my own experiences. What might or could-have happened is a lot of fun. For instance, a funny thing happened on my way to the mail box...

What do you like to do when you're not writing?
When not writing, I spend hours, days trying to get my computer, cell phone and digital watch to coordinate with my needs and work the way that I think they should. My requirements may not agree with the original intentions of the programmer, but I find that a martini (just wrapped myself around a sample) eases (without resolving) the conflicts.

As a child, what did you want to do when you grew up?
Too many interests to make a choice. In retrospect, perhaps becoming a professional Don Juan would have been a lot of fun. Instead, I became an engineer, although researching new explosives or studying to become a tail-gunner on an inner-city beer truck would have more exciting.

Heather Moser

Heather Moser

Where are you from?
A small town in eastern Ohio.

When and why did you begin writing?
I began writing poetry when I was a teenager in an attempt to deal with difficult emotions. I decided to start with poetry because my Dad writes love poems to my mother, and I admire that kind of affection. Constance was my first attempt at writing a short story.

What would you say is your most interesting writing quirk?
I save every version of and edit to my poetry I have ever written. I just cannot bring myself to discard my original poems because every word is deliberately chosen to capture a moment in time.

What do you like to do when you're not writing?
I love spending time with my family and researching anything related to ancient Rome.

As a child, what did you want to do when you grew up?
When I was a small child, a paleontologist. As an older child into early high school years, an astronomer. By my sophomore year of high school, I wanted to be a classicist.

Jennifer Koch

Jennifer Koch

Born in Galveston, Texas, Jennifer moved to Michigan when she was just a baby. An avid reader from elementary school on, she didn't start putting her own stories down on paper until early middle school. Her creative mind was active long before though, as evident in the tales of her neighbors who reminisce about a young girl who used to run around the neighborhood with friends and randomly put on plays that included both grand tales and amusing costumes. In developing her writing, she has become quite fond of characters and enjoys creating them as well as helping others develop their own. This strong desire to help others as well as learn about what makes them tick, is what lead her to a degree in psychology. Her storytelling preferences strongly favor deep internal conflict and character driven tales that focus on the grayness of morality.

Joann Grisetti

Joann Grisetti

Where are you from?
Joann lives in Florida with her husband and two sons.

When and why did you begin writing?
She began writing in her teens and has not stopped yet.

What would you say is your most interesting writing quirk?
Joann writes at any hour inspiration arrives, usually in the middle of the night.

What do you like to do when you're not writing?
She loves to go hiking and collects rocks during a trip to the western states every summer.

As a child, what did you want to do when you grew up?
Still trying to figure out what to do when she grows up, when will that be?

John Fitzpatrick

John Fitzpatrick

Where are you from?
Born in the Genesee River Valley village of Dansville, NY, home of Clara Barton and her 1st American Red Cross Chapter; now live in the Hudson River Valley village of equally historic Rhinebeck, NY, home of the Livingstons, the Beekmans, the Suckleys.

When and why did you begin writing?
I began writing poetry my senior year at the University of Notre Dame, for no specific reason.   Now I write poetry as a kind of catharsis, also because I've been blessed with a gift of communing with animal spirits that come to me uninvited—which resulted in my first published book, Moving To Completion, found on WEB: http://turtleami.com.

What would you say is your most interesting writing quirk?
Perhaps my habit of jotting ideas, experiences, lines, images on index cards, and paper scraps, then transferring them to computer which may or may not happen—its pluses and minuses.

What do you like to do when you're not writing?
I volunteer teach Kundalini Yoga to staff at Omega Institute for Holistic Studies, outside Rhinebeck, do Usui-Reiki, also Reconnective Healing TM work, plus commune with nature and animals.

As a child, what did you want to do when you grew up?
Since high school, intuitively knew I wanted to teach English which I later did, some 30 years at Hewlett High School, Long Island, NY, plus founded & coached a local, NY State, National award winning Speech-Debate Team. Now teach yoga, write poetry, give talks on communing with animals.

John J. Brugaletta

John J. Brugaletta

Where are you from?
The Northern California coast.

When and why did you begin writing?
I've always preferred meaningful talk over small talk, and there isn't always another introvert around when you need one.

What would you say is your most interesting writing quirk?
I usually write in bed.

What do you like to do when you're not writing?
Eat my wife's cooking, call friends, throw a tennis ball for my dog.

As a child, what did you want to do when you grew up?
Heal people.

Jon Moray

Where are you from?
Kissimmee, Florida

When and why did you begin writing?
I began writing 5 years ago because I felt I had good story ideas that should be read and not kept only to my imagination.

What would you say is your most interesting writing quirk?
My most interesting writing quirk is my desire to include a surprise twist ending, although most of my stories written do not.

What do you like to do when you're not writing?
I enjoy my time with my family, playing basketball and training for marathons.

As a child, what did you want to do when you grew up?
As a child I wanted to be a professional baseball player. The only problem was I couldn't hit, field or throw that well.

J. P. Christiansen

Where are you from?
Copenhagen, Denmark.

When and why did you begin writing?
Began writing as an adult after much traveling, roaming, seeking.
Words started pouring out, just.

What would you say is your most interesting writing quirk?
Quirk? Can't identify any. Is that quirky? I like the word "quirky";
tastes good. Rhymes with "murky", like my answer.

What do you like to do when you're not writing?
Read. Think. Meditate. Wait for poetry to announce itself in my
awareness, like a memory I forgot to register. Often wait years for
the right words and lines to shape themselves, by themselves. This
is the beauty of having poetry come when only it is ready.

As a child, what did you want to do when you grew up?
Can't remember. Now that I'm grown, I want to be a boy again.
Would like to try another version of life. Only poetry justifies the
years. Thank you for asking. Hope you didn't regret it.

K. W. DeWess

K. W. DeWess

Where are you from?
Rural Ogle Township in Somerset County, Pennsylvania is my home.

When and why did you begin writing?
Putting a story onto paper as soon as my hand could form letters for the words.   I'm a daydreamer and writing was a way of embellishing a favorite fantasy.

What would you say is your most interesting writing quirk?
It would be the tendency to associate a physical object with a story. For example, a pair of snowshoes serves as a talisman for 'Revelation.'

What do you like to do when you're not writing?
The wild things always beckon.   It is my good fortune to live where I can walk out the door into the wilderness and recharge my energy.

As a child, what did you want to do when you grew up?
My top choices were being a forest ranger; helping kids learn from history.

Kenneth Henry

Where are you from?
Carmel, Indiana.   I frequently post at Allpoetry.com under the name Ddoubletake.

When and why did you begin writing?
My first poem was written in third grade as a class assignment. It was about worms, which is one of the few acceptable topics for poetry for a third grade boy.

What would you say is your most interesting writing quirk?
I do my best writing within twenty minutes of my first cup of coffee in the morning.

What do you like to do when you're not writing?
Erase the crap I wrote the day before.

As a child, what did you want to do when you grew up?
In third grade, I told my teacher (yes, the same one who gave me the poetry assignment) that I wanted to be a marine microbiologist.

Mark Hudson

Mark Hudson

Where are you from?
Evanston, Illinois.

When and why did you begin writing?
I went to Columbia College in Chicago to study animation, because I'm an artist, but found It complicated, so I switched my major to fiction writing. I'm better at writing poetry than fiction, but do write stories when they come to me.

What would you say is your most interesting writing quirk?
My most interesting writing quirk is I don't know what a quirk is. And you can print that. Might as well add a little humor

What do you like to do when you're not writing?
I also draw, taking an art class at Noyes art center and a private portraiture class.

As a child, what did you want to do when you grew up?
My first goal was to be a garbage man. But then I didn't do well in high school, and ended Up with a lot of jobs dealing with taking out trash. Many artists I know had mundane jobs before they got their art education, and you appreciate being able to write and do art when you've had lousy jobs.

Michelle Cacho-Negrete

Michelle Cacho-Negrete

Where are you from?
Portland, Maine.

When and why did you begin writing?
I teach a class called sneaky politics - it's about making a political point without being polemic. I have strong feelings about certain things; ie - global climate change.   This is the best way to express them.

What would you say is your most interesting writing quirk?
Interesting - I'm not sure it's interesting, but I'm pretty obsessive about getting the exact wording for what I want to say.

What do you like to do when you're not writing?
I hike, junk shop, visit friends and grandchildren.

As a child, what did you want to do when you grew up?
A writer and a social worker - I've been able to do both.   I've had more than thirty publishing credits making my work both entertaining and informing readers.

I have had three essays selected for *The 100 Most Nnotable*, six *Pushcart* nominations; I am in *the Norton Anthology* and Thoreau's legacy through the Union of Concerned Scientists, as well as five other anthologies.   *UTNE* magazine called my essay, *In My House*, about George Bush and global climate change, "an example of great writing".   My essay on domestic violence, *In The Lion's Den*, won the *Hope Award*.   I've been in a number of literary magazines, with the bulk of my work in *The Sun*.   I edit/read for *Solstice* literary magazine.

Nasy Sankagiri

Nasy Sankagiri

Where are you from?
I was born and brought up in southern India, and came to the US as a graduate student. I've been living In Detroit metro area since 1997, working in automotive industry.

When and why did you begin writing?
I started writing in my mother tongue, Telugu, because I wanted to keep that connection alive. I started writing fiction because I felt that the Indian American community has some interesting stories to tell. Now, I want to tell those stories to wider audience.

What would you say is your most interesting writing quirk?
I find it easiest to write in first person stream of conscious, but I've learned that readers often find it irritating.

What do you like to do when you're not writing?
I am a man of many interests. I like long nature walks, listening to music (South Indian traditional music called Carnatic, and Jazz), visit museums, read, watch films and so on.

As a child, what did you want to do when you grew up?
I wanted to drive steam locomotives – I thought that was the most important job in the world.

Ruth Sabath Rosenthal

Ruth Sabath Rosenthal

Where are you from?
I'm originally from Philadelphia, PA, but have been a New Yorker for the better part of my life.

When and why did you begin writing?
I began writing in 1999, when I got my first computer, and concurrently signed up for my first poetry class. The rest is history.

What would you say is your most interesting writing quirk?
I only feel comfortable writing on a computer. Writing by hand feels very inhibiting, but I know that, for many poets, quite the opposite is true.

What do you like to do when you're not writing?
Reading great poetry, for me, is key to my own writing. I subscribe to some poetry newsletters and receive, via e-mail, wonderful poems each week, and the one's I particularly like, I save.

As a child, what did you want to do when you grew up?
I always imagined myself as married and a mother, which I did achieve. I never dreamed I'd, one day, be a published poet and author. Looking back, I'm as surprised as I think my parents would have been, had they lived to see the day.

RUTH SABATH ROSENTHAL is a New York poet, published in literary journals and poetry anthologies throughout the U.S. and Canada, Greece, India, Israel, Italy, Romania, and the U.K. In 2006, Ruth's poem "on yet another birthday" was nominated for a **Pushcart Prize**. She has three full-length books of poetry: "Facing Home and Beyond," "little, but by no means small," "Food: Nature vs. Nurture," and a chapbook "Facing Home."
www.ruthsabathrosenthal.moonfruit.com

Sarah Z. Sleeper

Sarah Z. Sleeper

Where are you from?
Lake Forest, Illinois and Walloon Lake, Michigan. I've also lived in Albuquerque, New Mexico, and Okinawa, Japan, and now live in Solana Beach, California.

When and why did you begin writing?
In grade school because I loved reading and admired authors.

What would you say is your most interesting writing quirk?
Quirk? Well, possibly that I'm a over-researcher. If I'm writing a 1,000 word essay, I might compile 75 or 100 pages of background research in the process. Or maybe my quirk is that I spend my writing and my evenings in the gym or on the tennis court. My creative work needs to be balanced by physical work.

What do you like to do when you're not writing?
Read, play tennis, work in animal rescue, spend time with family and friends, travel.

As a child, what did you want to do when you grew up?
Write for a living. And go to the Galapagos Islands. I've done both.

Taylor Burkard

Taylor Burkard

Where are you from?
Eau Claire, WI

What would you say is your most interesting writing quirk?
That I don't have any.

What do you like to do when you're not writing?
Watch wrestling and drink beer.

Yasmin Khan

Yasmin Khan

Where are you from?
Mumbai, India.

When and why did you begin writing?
As a child, I felt that bonding with nature and this inspired me to write poetry.

What would you say is your most interesting writing quirk?
It happens to me all the time, I think everything in life touches me in a unique way.

What do you like to do when you're not writing?
I go on long nature walks, listen to music.   I like to cook, too, and spend time with my family.

As a child, what did you want to do when you grew up?
I always wanted to be a writer.